THE MEDITATING PSYCHIATRIST WHO TRIED TO KILL HIMSELF

A Novel

Gudjon Bergmann

The Meditating Psychiatrist Who Tried to Kill Himself

Published by Flaming Leaf Press, 2016
www.flamingleafpress.com

ISBN 978-0-9973012-0-5

To Johanna

Chapter 1

"It's an attempted suicide case," Dr. Burns said on the phone. "We would like to consult with you."

"A suicide case?"

Robert Davis paced the floor in his office, weaving around the furniture, including two chairs, a desk, and a sofa for his clients. He had leased the space in January that year, moved into an affluent neighborhood in North Austin hoping to attract new customers. It was September already and thus far he had little to show for it.

"I am sorry Dr. Burns, but treating people who have attempted suicide is way outside of my expertise."

"We are aware of that," Dr. Burns replied, sounding slightly impatient, "but this case is special. We have looked around and you are one of a select few that can help us."

Robert was confused. He stopped pacing and looked out the window. This call, from a local mental hospital, had come out of nowhere. He knew of Dr. Andrew Burns—a highly respected and somewhat famous local psychiatrist that had been featured in *Scientific American Mind* and on *Good Morning America*—but had never met him.

"The patient is himself a psychiatrist," Dr. Burns continued, pressing the issue, waiting for Robert to respond.

How is that information supposed to help? It just puts the case further out of my reach, Robert thought to himself.

The knot in his stomach was tightening. He had gotten used to being at the bottom of the psychological pecking order, with psychiatrists at the top, followed by psychotherapists, then psychologists, down the line to counselors, and finally therapists like himself. It bothered him at first, not getting the respect he thought he deserved from his peers, but a few years ago he had decided to stop chasing that. He had decided that his commitment was to his clients, not to an irreverent elite. That made this phone call all the more surprising.

"What makes you think that I am the right person for the job?"

"Quite frankly, I am not sure that you are," Dr. Burns replied, "but we have a unique case on our hands. You see, the patient is not only a psychiatrist, but he has also been meditating for more than thirty years. In fact, his meditation practice may be the reason why he tried to commit suicide. Either way, he refuses to speak to anyone that has not been meditating for twenty years or more. He says that no one else will understand him. That's where you come in Mr. Davis. My assistant tells me that your profile fits the bill—that you have been meditating for more than twenty years. If that is correct, then that makes you one of the few people we know of here in Austin, who have both a therapy background and meditative experience."

More than twenty years?

Right, that's what it said on the website, wasn't it?

See what you've gotten yourself into, Robert scolded himself mentally. You shouldn't lie. Not even a little.

Robert's meditation practice had been fairly stable for the last five years, but consistent over a period of twenty? No. Not every day. Not even every other day. There had been long pauses in between. Nevertheless, he counted his inconsistent practice as full twenty years, both on his website and LinkedIn profile. He did it purely for marketing purposes. The embellishment was meant for his clients, not for the psychiatric community at large—certainly not for Dr. Burns.

What a precarious position. Robert could not refute the information that he had put out there as part of his public persona, especially not if the celebrity-like psychiatrist on the phone believed it. Claiming full twenty years was an exaggeration rather than a straight out lie, but if he turned around now and told the truth, it would tarnish the reputation that he had spent the last few years creating. With business being as slow as it was, he couldn't afford that.

Say something. Answer the man.

"Yes, that is correct," Robert finally answered after a long pause. "Meditation has been a part of my routine for over twenty years now and I teach some classes, but I still don't understand. Why do you want me to consult?"

"Two reasons," Dr. Burns answered, his impatience becoming more evident. It was clear that he was not used to asking for help. "First, in every other way the patient seems to be sane. Although he is not being co-operative, he displays none of the characteristics common to suicidal patients. Second, as I mentioned before, he hardly talks to us. When pressed, he says we are not worthy, that he will only speak to someone who understands him. The analogy he uses is that we wouldn't expect an algebra genius to talk about the finer aspects of math with someone who doesn't know the multiplication table."

The doctor paused and sighed.

"Look, Mr. Davis. I am not sure that it will work, and, in all honesty, I am hesitant about consulting with you, but we are curious to see if you can get him to talk, to see if he will open up to you. The question is: Will you take the job?"

Robert thought about all the reasons why he shouldn't do this. He knew he wasn't good enough, neither as a meditator nor as a therapist, but the lack of competency had not stopped him in the past. He had often faked it and succeeded. Yet, something told him that this time it could be different. He was playing at a higher level.

On the other hand, he was curious. Ever since the phone call began, a question had been ringing in his mind. Why would anyone who has been meditating for this long try to kill himself? It was a compelling mystery. If he could solve it, then... well, it would go down as a major accomplishment on his resume.

Plus, consulting with the mental hospital could mean a boost for his business. Getting a stamp of approval as a consultant to the well-known Dr. Burns at the Austin Psychiatric Hospital could lead to more consulting jobs. It could even mean more money for each client he saw.

Say yes. Take the job, an eager voice in his head whispered.

"Okay," Robert answered. "I'll do it. When do you want me to come in?"

"Tomorrow, if you can. 9 AM."

"I'll be there," Robert replied, without even discussing fees.

He felt a sudden surge of energy. His heart thumping. His fingers shaking ever so slightly. It was fear combined with excitement—the good kind of stress—or that was how he had conditioned himself to think about it. Yes. It was the good kind of stress.

Chapter 2

That night, Robert's meditation practice was sketchy, to say the least. Short moments of peace were crowded out by thoughts about his consultation tomorrow and frequent interruptions from his wife, Jessica.

Every night he would attempt to sit for ten to thirty minutes in their bedroom, cross-legged on top of two Mexican blankets and a red meditation cushion. He was no longer torturing himself by attempting a full lotus pose. Quite frankly, he didn't know which pained him more, the thought of all the years he spent trying to twist his legs into a pretzel or the actual pain in his knee from damaging it due to his efforts. These days he focused on sitting in comfort. Keeping his back straight and maintaining alert awareness was more important than the position of his legs. Sometimes, he even sat on a chair.

When he'd begun practicing this routine on a regular basis, five years ago, Robert had waited for Jessica to get into bed before he sat down, but their nightly schedules were so wildly different that he would sometimes spend more time waiting for her than he would on the actual meditation practice.

She was considerate—that wasn't the problem—but, as he sat, he would hear everything she did while preparing for bed. From brushing her teeth to her walking back and forth to get water or change the AC settings or check on the kids, from her flushing the toilet to her getting into bed and leafing through her books.

Sometimes these minuscule sounds would not bother him one bit. Other times they would irritate him in the same way that a dripping sink can be more bothersome than the continuous sound of traffic. Tonight, he was wound up, extra sensitive, easily irritated by everything. It was hard not to think about tomorrow's consultation and its implications.

There was a strict doctor-patient confidentiality clause in the agreement that had been emailed to Robert after his talk with Dr. Burns, underscoring the sensitivity of the case. Robert couldn't say a word to his wife. Not a word. The confidentiality boundary was more fluid in his personal therapy practice. He talked to Jessica about his cases all the time. Sometimes she gave him key insights when he was stuck. She had helped him through his studies after all. This time, though, he was muted. Alone. All he could tell her was that he had gotten a consulting job.

From the hospital email, Robert had learned that the patient's name was Dr. Vigo Andersen, a sixty-two-year-old man who had no family in the USA. His mother had emigrated with him from Norway but had died when he was in college. Prior to his suicide attempt, Dr. Andersen's psychiatry practice had been small, just enough to sustain him. He had spent most of his free time meditating.

That struck Robert as a complete paradox. How could someone's life be devoted to a meditation practice and legal drug pushing at the same time? It didn't make any sense. Then again, neither did this case.

Robert's initial excitement about the opportunity had been waning ever since he got the phone call, just before noon. Self-doubt had chipped away at his confidence as the day wore on. As he sat on his meditation cushion, supposedly getting ready to elicit peace, questions assailed his mind, blinking like neon-colored signs for a cheap motel: *Why did I take this case? How am I supposed to help this guy?*

To quell his doubts, Robert rearranged his legs, sat up straight, and tried to focus on his mantra.

One. One. One. One.

Tap turned on. Brushing sound. Tap turned off.

Temporary distraction. Back to the mantra.

One. One. One. One.

Breathing slowed.

Body calmed down.

One. One. One.

Moment of peace… but not for long.

Irritation, fear, and anxiety all bubbled to the surface. His insecurities screamed in chorus: What are you doing? You are lying through your teeth about your meditation practice. Don't you think that Dr. Andersen could be lucid enough to realize that? Are you sure that Dr. Burns won't demand proof of your abilities?

Calm down, Robert commanded himself, trying to summon his voice of reason. You don't need to worry. Just talk to him like a human being. Talk and listen. That is how you have helped people. That is why people come to you. That is how you solve things. He is human. You are a human. He has a problem. You want to help. Be sincere. Talk and listen. Listen and talk. Do what you can. And don't be worried about either of them noticing your lack of experience. You are a master of creating a calm exterior, even when your mind is racing. Just like now. Your body is completely still and no one can see what is going on in your mind.

That's right. My body is still. My body is calm. No one can see my mind. I'll be fine.

He turned his attention turned back to his mantra.

One. One. One. One.

Sensation of peace.

One. One. One.

Breathing slowed, almost to a standstill.

Body relaxed.

Prolonged moment of deep peace.

One. One.

Toilet flushing.

Let go of all distractions.

One.

Absolute calm. Absolute peace.

Damn. My knee is hurting again.

Chapter 3

Why did they have to argue this morning? Any other day would have been fine, but today? It wasn't fair.

Robert sat in his car — still in the driveway of their one-story stone house in Northwest Austin — and tried to refocus. He had gotten upset when Jessica kept reminding him of all the things that he needed to do that day.

Pick up the kids. Yes. Go grocery shopping. Yes. Clean the house. Really? Do you have to tell me to do that? Don't be like that Robert. I am going to be busy all day.

Jessica made most of the money in their relationship and that made her job more important than his. His role was to be the lead parent — a fancy name for being the housekeeper and primary babysitter — and he was okay with that, but he couldn't stand it when she reminded him of his duties. He didn't need reminding. It made him feel like she was his mother rather than his wife; made him feel like his business wasn't important. Sure, it was struggling, but it still had the possibility of becoming a viable business. Sometimes she spoke about it as a hobby. That was why they had argued.

This morning, though, Robert wasn't just angry at Jessica. He was angry at himself for getting upset in the first place. It was the burden of being a therapist. He should've known better. Why couldn't he just have let it go? It was nothing.

Emotions are like the weather, Robert reminded himself. They will pass.

He took one deep breath, then another deep breath.

I hope they pass soon. I need to be ready for the consultation.

Robert started the engine of his car, a decade old, shimmering, silver Mercury Grand Marquis in pristine condition and the radio came on.

"You are listening to KUT, your local NPR station. The time is 8 AM. Currently, it is eighty degrees at Camp Mabry. Expect a high today of one hundred and three. We thank you for listening. Now, the news."

The voice of Bob Branson had a calming effect.

At least, we didn't argue in front of the kids, Robert thought, trying to put a positive spin on what had happened. Their morning routine had been perfect if not for the argument, a textbook example of seamless parental cooperation.

Feeling slightly better, Robert decided that it was time to venture into the notorious Austin traffic. The drive from his home to the Austin Psychiatric Hospital could take anywhere from thirty to forty-five minutes during rush hour—fifteen minutes with no traffic. He should be alright. He had an hour to work with.

The sound of KUT kept Robert company as he headed towards his destination. To him, the ability to listen to public radio was nearly as calming as his meditation practice. The down to earth news reporting was a pleasant relief from the political extremes of cable TV and the unnecessary hype of local news.

After the 8 AM news, KUT featured a story about water preservation efforts in Austin. It described battles with rice farmers that used water from the Lower Colorado River for their water-intensive irrigation. Using water for rice farming in Texas—a state famous for its droughts—was evidently ill-advised, but instead of changing that, Austinites were being asked to drastically reduce their water consumption.

The station then aired two interviews. One with a political commentator about the low voter turnout expected in the midterm elections—no surprise—and another with a sports commentator about NFL concussions and the prospects for the baseball postseason.

When the business news came on at 8.30 AM, Robert realized that he had only gotten halfway to his destination. The line of cars on Mopac was bumper to bumper as far as the eye could see.

Was leaving an hour early for a trip that took fifteen minutes without traffic not enough anymore? In frustration, Robert raised his hand to honk the horn but immediately realized that it wouldn't have any effect.

He looked at the clock again. It was now 8.35 AM. His grandmother's mantra rang in his ears. If you're on time, you're late. Better to be early, Robert. Yes Nana, but you don't know the Austin traffic. The roads here weren't built to handle all these cars.

To Robert's immense relief, the traffic got rolling just as he passed the 45th Street exit. He took the Enfield exit, weaved his way through the side streets, and arrived at the Austin Psychiatric Hospital just in time, at 8.55 AM.

He parked in the first available parking spot he found. All the shady parking spots were already taken so he was forced to park directly in the sun. He took the keys out of the ignition and turned around in his seat to look for the front window shade. Damn. He'd left it in Jessica's car. With temperatures in the hundreds, the steering wheel would be blistering hot when he came out of the hospital. He felt like he was going to boil over. Couldn't anything go right this morning?

Stay focused, he told himself. The heat is just part of living in Austin—better that than the continual cloudiness and rain in Seattle. Let it go. It's time to get moving.

With tunnel vision, he opened the car door and headed for the hospital entrance, hardly noticing his surroundings. The foyer was busy and the sounds of high heels and dress shoes clicking on the tiled floor caught Robert's attention as he walked into the sterilized gray and wood paneled hospital environment. The Austin Psychiatric Hospital certainly looked like the high-end version of a mental facility, one in which a minimalist architect had gotten free reign judging by the look and feel of the building materials.

A blonde, perky girl at the reception desk, whose nametag read Amanda, greeted Robert with Southern niceties and a wide smile as he approached.

"Good morning. How's your day been going so far?"

"Fine, thank you," Robert responded, tension reverberating in his voice. "My name is Mr. Davis. I am here to see Dr. Burns."

"Right down the hall sweetie. Take the elevator. Second floor, then to the right."

As Robert hurried towards his destination, he passed one white-coated doctor after another. They were men and women of knowledge, prestige, and trustworthiness; at least, that was what he imagined. Each and every one of them seemed to be locked in, on a mission, going somewhere. Robert felt a familiar pang in his stomach. His degree didn't match theirs. Not even close.

I should've dressed up, he thought, looking down on his khaki pants, polo shirt, and dress shoes, all black, for slimming purposes. His nerves were relentless. He was light years outside of his comfort zone. He tried to revive his confidence by mentally repeating the words, I am human, they are human, I am human, they are human...

"Please sign these papers sir and then take a seat. I will show you in momentarily," said Karen Bundy, the doctor's nerdy, brunette, wound-up assistant.

She was probably the one who had found Robert online.

For a moment, Robert wished she hadn't.

Chapter 4

Dr. Burns looked exactly like he did in his pictures, a tall, white man, with shortly trimmed silver hair and beard, blue shirt, red power tie, white robe, and black-rimmed glasses. His deep blue eyes were intense, yet calm. He was authority in the flesh. His handshake was firm and his manner confident. He made Robert feel like he was back in grade school.

"Glad to meet you, Mr. Davis."

"The honor is all mine, Dr. Burns."

"I thought we could take a few minutes to set up expectations before I take you to see the patient if that is alright with you," Dr. Burns said, as he sat down in his plush chair. His bookshelves were lined with gilded, leather bound psychology textbooks. His walls were covered with certificates.

Robert thought back to his own office where he only had two certificates and a small bookshelf stacked with paperbacks. This office was three times the size of his.

Stop comparing. I am human, he is human.

"Of course, I'd *expect* nothing less," Robert said with a smile and a nervous chuckle, referring to the expectation setting, trying to lighten the mood and sound confident. But his play on words didn't elicit a response from the good doctor.

"Have you gone over the paperwork with my assistant?" Dr. Burns asked, pretending like he had not heard the attempted quip.

"Yes, everything is signed. I am fine with the fee for today, but we may need to renegotiate if I am to come in on a regular basis," Robert replied as he sat down in the chair facing Dr. Burns.

"Yes, yes, of course, but for today your goals are simple. You are here to consult because of your meditation expertise and... "

Dr. Burns stopped talking. He looked distracted as he searched through the paperwork on his desk. The silence created a tense moment. Then, as if woken from a daydream, the doctor shook his head, straightened his back, raised his eyes to meet Robert's gaze and continued.

"Mr. Davis, as you know, Dr. Andersen has refused to talk to anyone who doesn't have experience with meditation. All we know about his reasons is that when he was being resuscitated, half lucid because of the drugs he had taken, he cried, and let me read from his file here: No! I am still in the dream. Please stop. Let me wake up. We don't know exactly what he meant by that… which is partly why you are here."

Dr. Burns cleared his throat.

"Your goal Mr. Davis, as our guest consultant here today, is two-fold. First, you need to convince the patient, Dr. Andersen, that you have the experience that you say you have. I don't know how you will do that exactly, how you will get him to trust you, and therefore, that part is completely up to you. Second, you need to get him to talk. That is imperative. We cannot possibly make any progress if he remains silent."

"Got it. Convince him that I have meditation experience and get him to talk."

Robert tried to sound chipper, even as he weighed the odds, which were clearly stacked against him. A collision of low competency with an overwhelming task was about to happen, yet Robert pushed forward. He was here. There was no turning back.

"Is there anything special I need to know?" Robert asked with all the confidence he could muster.

"Have you ever been engaged with a patient who is on the suicidal watch?"

"No, as I told you on the phone, I have no experience when it comes to suicides."

"It's common sense really. Don't mention the suicide attempt directly and don't bring any sharp objects with you or leave clothing items that could be fashioned into a noose. We don't anticipate any problems. Dr. Andersen seems to want to go peacefully. He took pills and was caught just in time, so I don't expect him to elevate his game and try anything violent, but as with all procedures, it is better to be safe than sorry. We have a reputation to uphold."

"Yes, of course," Robert replied.

"Do you have any questions or are you ready to get started?" Dr. Burns asked as he got up and prepared to walk Robert to the door.

"No questions sir," Robert replied, also standing up. "I am ready and eager to get started."

As the two of them walked towards the door, Dr. Burns added: "You know Mr. Davis, for reasons I cannot divulge, this case is especially important to me. Any progress that can be made today would be better than this."

"Understood sir," Robert answered as he straightened his back, "I will do my best."

"Yes, yes, of course," Dr. Burns replied. Then he sighed as if he didn't believe it would be good enough.

Chapter 5

The shiny, white, linoleum-floored room was exceedingly well-lit, to the point of hurting the eyes. In it were none of the posh wood and metal elements that characterized the halls.

When Robert walked in, he saw Dr. Vigo Andersen sitting on a twin bed, cross-legged, in a textbook meditation pose if he'd ever seen one. He was a man of medium build, slightly overweight and completely bald, except for two or three days' worth of silver stubble on his head and face. He was wearing all white, a robe, t-shirt, and baggy pants. He seemed calm and happy. His eyes were closed, his forehead smooth, and the sides of his mouth were slightly turned up—almost like he was smiling to himself. He reminded Robert of Laughing Buddha depictions he had seen over the years.

"Excuse me, Dr. Andersen?" Robert said tentatively.

No response. No movement. Only calm. Stillness.

"Dr. Andersen?"

Nothing stirred. Nothing happened.

Robert looked around the room. There was nothing in there except for one bed and two chairs. No pictures on the walls. No decorations of any kind. The smell was of hospital sanitation. There were two tinted windows on either side of the door through which he had entered; windows that were used by the staff for observation.

"My name is Robert Davis. I am a therapist. I have more than twenty years of meditative experience. I am told that you will speak with no one unless they have that kind of experience. Is that right?"

No reaction. If not for a slight breathing movement, Robert would have assumed that Dr. Andersen was already dead.

That's impressive, Robert thought, I usually twitch in response to minor movements in my surroundings when I am meditating, but here he is, sitting peacefully, not even the slightest movement.

"Dr. Andersen?" Robert tried again.

Nothing.

One more time, with more force—the kind that Robert employed when he was correcting his children and regretted raising his voice too much.

"Dr. Andersen!?"

Again, no response.

Robert sat on one of the padded chairs, watching Dr. Andersen intently. The doctor was obviously in a deep state of meditation. There was no movement, not even in the eyes.

Okay, think Robert, think!

He weighed his options. He could raise his voice even more or try some kind of kinetic stimulation, touching, but that might backfire and it probably wouldn't convince Dr. Andersen that Robert was worth talking to. He could sit here and watch him, wait until he came out of his meditation, but that wouldn't work either. There were time restraints. If Robert didn't show any progress today, then maybe, there would be no trying again tomorrow.

Think dammit, think! He is a human. You are a human.

Robert revisited his meditation training. In the early days, he had tried several techniques until he settled on the simple one he had stuck with since.

Initially, he had trained with Father Martin, a Catholic priest in Seattle, who had emphasized sitting in the silence, repeating a mantra mentally, and then speaking about the experience of being immersed in spirit, as the priest had called it. The Catholic mantra was *Maranatha*, which meant Come Lord. Robert had soon realized that he wasn't religious enough to participate. After several heated theological debates with the priest, he had decided that the Catholic meditation approach wasn't for him.

The Zen monks he had studied with after that were much stricter in comparison. In fact, their intense discipline had pushed Robert away, probably because of his deep seeded authority resistance.

Sit still. Look at the wall, they would say. He could never get used to being hit with a stick when he was slouching.

The good thing about their approach, however, was that they were meticulous in testing the progress of their students. They tested while both the student and teacher attempted to meditate near each other. Robert had never quite figured out how they did it, but the monks seemed to have ways of measuring states of consciousness. Maybe they sensed changes in movement and breathing. Maybe they sensed changes in energy. Robert didn't know. He doubted that the monks could read students minds, but whatever they did, it seemed to work. The Zen students slowly moved through stages of meditation depending on the feedback they got from their teachers.

While he thought about what to do, Robert observed Dr. Andersen carefully. Based on both what he had learned in the past and the few minutes he had spent monitoring this old psychiatrist—his peaceful posture, near non-existent breathing, and lack of movement—Robert surmised that he was probably in the presence of an advanced meditator, whatever else was wrong with him. In comparison, Robert was an absolute beginner. He was the student and Dr. Andersen the master. Maybe that was the way to approach him. As a beginner. As a student.

Okay, but how?

With the Zen monks, the student needed to prove himself. But, it was more than that. If Robert were to convince Dr. Andersen to talk to him, he would need to demonstrate that the student was equal to the master. Dr. Andersen was looking for an equal, someone that would understand him.

Yes, Robert thought, he wants a peer. At least, that's the best I can come up with. He is looking for a peer and I need to prove myself as one. I need to get into a deep state of meditation and hope that he notices.

It was a daring plan, to say the least. Robert knew that Dr. Burns and his colleagues were watching from behind the tinted windows, meticulously writing down everything that they saw. He knew that he was taking a chance, but this was why they had brought him in. He was the meditating therapist. He needed to prove himself as such.

Okay, this is it, his internal pep talk continued. You can do this Robert. Let go of everything and be in the moment. Let go of expectations. Let go of the outcome. This day will be what it will be. You are only part of the picture. If he accepts you as a peer, great. If not, you need to be alright with that as well.

He looked at his phone. The time was 9:37 AM. Time to meditate.

For Robert, the process of entering the meditative state always began with the posture—with getting comfortable. For this session, he decided to stay in his chair, no fancy cross-legged stuff. His spine was straight, his feet planted firmly on the floor. He rotated his neck a few times, took several deep breaths and shook out his arms. He had no idea for how long he needed to sit still, but his body needed to be mostly tension-free. He went through the methodical relaxation process that he had practiced so often before. Relax the body step by step—not too much, don't slump. Then, ten deep breaths, slowing down with each exhalation.

At the end of that process, Robert's body was calm, but his mind was still racing. Of course, the onlookers would see no evidence of that. They would only see the calm surface, and yet, Robert knew that it wasn't enough. What if Dr. Andersen could really sense consciousness?

Slow down the mind. Let go of all thoughts except one…
One. One. One. One.
With every heartbeat.
One. One. One.
Now, slower, with every inhale and every exhale.
One. One.
Slower.
One…
Finally, a moment of peace.
Is he awake? Is he looking at me? Are they looking at me?
Let go of thoughts. Focus on the mantra.
To the rhythm of the heart.
One. One. One. One.
Slower, with the breath.
One. One. One.
Slower.

One…
Moment of peace.
Deep peace.

Chapter 6

"Mr. Davis," an unfamiliar voice interrupted, "I am ready to talk now."

Robert opened his eyes slowly. It was Dr. Andersen.

Success! He was talking.

Robert looked at his phone again. The time was now 10:21 AM. He had been sitting still for forty-four minutes. He was slightly disoriented and his body felt lifeless. After stretching and taking a couple of deep breaths to revitalize himself, he looked up at Dr. Andersen who still sat motionless on the bed, but now his emerald green eyes were open and he was smiling broadly.

"You haven't really been meditating for more than twenty years, have you?" Dr. Andersen asked.

Robert was startled by the question, although he was still trying to fully regain his awareness. He felt self-conscious like someone had caught him in the nude.

"No," he answered in a low, hoarse voice as if he didn't want the onlookers to hear what he said. His vocal chords were rusty as if he had just woken up from a long night's sleep.

"You did well. You went deep."

"Thank you?" Robert answered, still disoriented.

It was true. He had seldom gone as deep into the meditative state. It was a definite breakthrough. He had pushed himself to the brink, taken a leap of faith and broken through an internal barrier. During his nightly practice, he hardly ever pushed himself, never ventured into the deep. Rather, he was content with short moments of peace.

"How did you know?" Robert asked, wondering both, how Dr. Andersen knew that he hadn't been meditating consistently for twenty years, and, how he knew that Robert had gone deep into the meditative state.

"No matter," Dr. Andersen answered in a pleasing voice, still smiling. "Why did you start meditating?"

After being exposed for his lack of experience, Robert felt vulnerable. In a weird way, he couldn't help but entertain the idea that this man, who had recently attempted to commit suicide, was some sort of meditation master. Suicidal or not, Dr. Andersen was certainly able to enter deep states of altered consciousness. It was eerie, to say the least, and now, Robert couldn't imagine telling him a lie—he felt as if Dr. Andersen could see right through him.

"I started meditating because I quit drinking, because I am an alcoholic. It was something that was suggested in the twelve step program," he answered truthfully.

"So—your reason was pain," Dr. Andersen replied calmly. "And you were looking for happiness, yes?" he added, sounding like he had both made a statement and asked a question at the same time.

Robert knew that he was the one who was supposed to get Dr. Andersen to talk, not the other way around, but he felt compelled to respond. Maybe the doctor would reciprocate.

"Yes and no," Robert answered, shifting in his chair, straightening his back, trying to somehow make himself appear a little more respectable, less vulnerable. "I just wanted to experience moments of peace, to quiet my mind, even if it was temporary. I was a mess, unable to control my thoughts or emotions. Meditation was one of the things that helped. It made me happier at times, but never completely happy—I mean, I never expected it to."

There was a short pause.

When Dr. Andersen didn't respond, Robert continued.

"All in all, meditation has made me a little less irritated. I enjoy more moments of peace. I look at it as my reset button. My wife comments if I skip the practice for a few days—says that my fuse becomes shorter."

Robert was about to dive into a more elaborate reverie and expose more of what meditation had done for him. It felt like a dam was about to break—just like what would happen with his clients when he asked open-ended questions and leaned back and said nothing—but he caught himself just in time and stopped.

For a couple of minutes, Robert and Dr. Andersen just looked at each other and said nothing, like they were in a fifth-grade staring contest.

"I am not sick," Dr. Andersen finally said in a firm, calm voice, his green eyes serene.

"Is that why you wanted to meet with someone who could meditate Dr. Andersen? To tell them that?" Robert hesitantly asked, considering himself lucky to finally get a question in edgewise.

"How would you describe the state you were in a few minutes ago?" Dr. Andersen asked, without answering Robert's question.

"As deep peace," Robert answered without thinking.

"Was it real to you?"

"Yes, the peace was real."

"Which state would you consider reality, the state you are in now or the state you were in before?" Dr. Andersen asked.

It felt like the older man was looking straight into Robert's soul.

"What do you mean?" Robert asked, sincerely confused. "This, here, right now, this is reality. The other state, meditation, that is an altered state of consciousness."

"You are wrong about that, you know," Dr. Andersen replied calmly. "This, right here—us talking, sitting in this overlit room, a bunch of shrinks watching us through the tinted windows—this is the dream. The peace you felt before, that is reality. It is the I. The only part of existence that does not change, that cannot change, that will not change. You may not be ready to understand this quite yet, but if you continue meditating, you will."

Looking at the clock on his phone, Robert realized that he had been in the room with Dr. Andersen for more than an hour. Knowing that his time was nearly up, he decided to go out on a limb, to push the envelope a little.

"Well, if that is the end result, then I am not sure if I want to continue meditating. How can you even think that this, our everyday waking consciousness, is a dream?" Robert asked probingly, hoping for a response, but instead, he got a rubber wall—nothing.

Maybe I need to create a confrontation, Robert thought, his NLP training kicking in. What was it that they always said; when the record is spinning on the same track, scratch it, do something unexpected, push their buttons, get them out of their comfort zone.

"Is that why you tried to kill yourself?" Robert asked in an adversarial tone, breaking the one guideline given to him by Dr. Burns. "Were you trying to fulfill an idealistic concept of everlasting peace?"

He paused for effect, then turned up the heat and went straight for what he thought was the soft spot.

"I mean, if that's why you did it, if that's why you tried to kill yourself, to be in some sort of eternal bliss, then you are just as delusional as the jihadists who commit suicide expecting to end in paradise with forty virgins."

Robert knew that his approach would likely be frowned upon by Dr. Burns and his staff, that it would probably disqualify him from further consultations, yet, he felt vindicated, like he had broken through all the bullshit and spoken the truth—his truth.

There was silence.

Then, out of nowhere, Dr. Andersen began laughing. Not like a crazy person, but heartily, like he had just been told the funniest joke he'd ever heard. The laugh was deep, sincere, and kept magnifying, moment to moment, expanding, deepening, booming, becoming louder and louder. Dr. Andersen shook and rolled back and forth. Tears started rolling down his cheeks.

Robert was astounded at first, shocked really, but after a while, the laughter began resonating. It was contagious and genuine. There was nothing funny about the situation, but Robert started giggling as well, and within a minute or so, both men were laughing hard. Tears were streaming down their cheeks. Their bodies shook, almost in rhythm.

Then, Dr. Andersen stopped laughing as abruptly as he had begun and regained his smiling, calm composure. It took a moment for Robert to realize that he was now the only one laughing. He stopped with some effort and tried to act professionally, but he knew that he had blown it with the onlookers. He wouldn't be asked to come here again.

With damp eyes, the two men looked at each other. Dr. Andersen, who was still sitting in a lotus pose, leaned slightly forward and spoke in a slow, methodical tone, keeping eye contact with Robert the entire time.

"Know this Mr. Davis. I am not crazy. I am not sane. I am not alive. I am not dead. I am not even the human being who you call Dr. Vigo Andersen. I was never born and I will never die. I am an eternal being. *I am that I am.* This, what you call reality, is just a collective dream. I was about to wake up from it permanently when I was yanked back into this temporal space. I did not try to kill myself. I tried to wake up."

Dr. Andersen said these words with such depth, such sincerity that even though Robert had heard some of it before — and properly dismissed it as primitive philosophy — now, at this moment, with what he had just experienced, nothing he had ever heard before seemed as real. Could it be? Was the peace reality and everything else just a mirage?

Robert shook his head. No. That can't be.

The doctor continued: "This mental hospital is not real. Reality is one, not many. It was my time to wake up, to make my transition. Your intervention is just temporary. My transition cannot be stopped. I will wake up from this dream and be in reality, be in peace. The same is true for you. You felt it before. Peace is reality. It is the unchanging I. The ever-changing sensory world is the illusion. It is the people who believe in that illusion who are really insane."

The two men sat in silence, looking deeply into each other's eyes.

The peace is reality? Everything else is a dream? Really?

The door opened abruptly.

"Mr. Davis," Dr. Burns said as he entered the room. "Thank you for your help. Your session with Dr. Andersen is now over."

As they walked to the elevator, there was no mention of Robert's unconventional techniques. Dr. Burns thanked him for his help and said that they would call if they needed his services again.

Chapter 7

Although Robert was in a state of utter confusion when he arrived at his office, it only took one glance at his 1 PM client for him to guess her type. Her name was Melissa Rodgers, a local project manager in her early thirties. She was wearing active wear and had probably done some sort of exercise during her lunch break. Nevertheless, she didn't look very healthy and was evidently underweight. Robert guessed that she most likely obsessed about her diet, eating exclusively at places like Whole Foods and Central Market, and was either a marathon runner or a hot yoga practitioner—maybe both. However she did it, she most definitely tried to control everything about her body and environment to mask the fact that her thoughts and emotions constantly felt out of control.

Besides his treatment of alcoholics, her type was one of the reasons why Robert stayed in business. On the surface, it looked like she had everything under control, but underneath, her emotional life was a mess. Robert had even bought a picture to illustrate this problem and hung it on the wall in his office. It was a black and white cartoon of a duck swimming on a pond. It showed the motionless body above water and the webbed feet working frantically below the surface. The captioning said: *Calm on the surface, paddling like crazy underneath.*

Some of his clients interpreted the picture by saying that they should keep calm and carry on but what the picture really referred to was the internal mental and emotional turmoil that many people felt while they displayed a calm surface. Robert described it as the poker face of emotional pain. He knew it all too well from personal experience. Sometimes he spoke about it the past tense, but in reality, the paddling-like-crazy-poker-face was still very much a part of him.

Robert knew that he shouldn't judge a book by its cover—that he should aspire to be more professional—but based on his track record, he had begun to consider himself as somewhat of a psychological

Sherlock. He would probably do better in Vegas if it were possible to bet on emotional types rather than sports. After speaking to Melissa for a few minutes, his initial guesswork was confirmed... or close enough.

Melissa was having panic attacks. Her heart rate was elevated, even when she tried to relax. She experienced emotional outbursts at inappropriate times and she was often out of breath. Her physician had found nothing physically wrong with her. A few weeks ago, she had talked to a psychiatrist for about ten minutes and he immediately wanted to put her on meds. She didn't want that, no drugs please, she'd said, I prefer natural solutions. She had heard about Robert from a woman in a similar situation.

While Melissa spoke, describing her circumstances in detail, Robert couldn't stop thinking about Dr. Andersen. What peace. What calm. Even when Robert had tried to provoke him. What depth.

Wait a minute, the reasonable voice in his head retorted. He tried to kill himself. There is no way around that part of the story. It doesn't compute. Why would a person, that seems so much at peace, want to exit this life? He can't seriously think that the peace will continue, can he?

"Can you help me?"

Robert had been staring at the wall above Melissa, lost in thought, and was pulled back into the moment when she asked the question.

Could he help her? Could he?

If anyone had asked him the same question twenty-four hours ago, they would have gotten a definite yes, but now...

He quickly scanned the usual remedies. Deep breathing techniques. Simple tensing and relaxing exercises. Forgiveness work. Time management skills. Life balance. Meditation. He knew that anyone who looked closely enough at his practice could see that despite everything he had learned in college he still used more of what he had learned in the twelve step program with his clients than anything else. He didn't care where he got his methods from; he only cared whether or not they worked. His goal was to help people to help themselves, to encourage self-reliance, not to chain people to endless therapy sessions. Overall, his approach was good for his clients, at least, the ones who followed his advice, but no doubt it was bad for business.

You have to set up your practice so that people keep coming back, his peers had said many times.

Robert didn't believe that. He believed in solutions. Permanent solutions.

Yet, her question remained.

Could he help her?

Today, he wasn't entirely sure.

What if I teach her breathing, relaxation, and meditation… and then she tries to kill herself?

Come on, the reasonable voice in his head responded forcefully. Isn't that going too far? You've been helping people for years now, doing these exact same things, and not one of them has tried to kill themselves. Not one! In fact, most of them have reported great benefits, especially in the form of tension relief, and let's face it, tension relief is the best most people can hope for. Of course you can help her.

What about the deep peace I felt this morning? Will that eventually lead me to want to die as well? Will I end up talking about dying as wanting to wake up from the dream of life, just like Dr. Andersen did? Am I setting people on a path that will eventually lead them to prefer death?

Snap out of it, the reasonable voice once again responded, evidently fed up with this internal self-doubting. Teach this girl some breathing techniques. Help her in the same way that you have helped others.

Chapter 8

Robert arrived at his children's one story, brick elementary school just before 2.45 PM. The line of cars was almost a mile long by then. He could have gotten there sooner, but after Melissa had left, he'd remained motionless in his leather chair, stunned by the day's events. If not for a call from Jessica—wanting to add green tea to the shopping list—he would've been late. He still didn't feel quite right.

As he waited in line, Robert observed the teachers working outside, helping the kids get into their parent's cars in the blistering hundred-degree heat. They looked uncomfortable, to say the least, but still, they smiled, assisted the kids, and said have a nice day to the parents.

Sacrifice, the thought to himself. Another word for which was love, as Scott Peck, his favorite author, had defined it. Love, Peck had said, is the willingness to sacrifice of one's time, energy and money, to help another person grow.

Robert loved his kids. He sacrificed for them, gladly.

From what he saw, the teachers loved the children they served as well, especially when he considered what they were being paid.

It was 3 PM before he got to the front of the line. James, his ten-year-old, and Cathy, his five-year-old, got into the car, their faces red and hairlines sweaty from waiting longer than usual in the heat.

"Hey kiddos," Robert greeted them. "How was school?"

"Good," they responded in unison.

They loved going to school. Imagine that. He wished that he had gotten the same kind of support when he was growing up, both from his parents and from his teachers. His life would have turned out quite differently. But his leash had been too long and the temptations too many. Useless regrets.

Instead of his usual after school routine—following up by asking for specifics, such as, what had been good about school and getting to know more about the teachers and the children's friends—Robert said nothing.

"Can we listen to the radio, daddy?" the little one asked enthusiastically. "96.7?"

She knew the dial. It was the local pop music station—the kind of music that Robert wouldn't have been caught dead listening to in his teens and early twenties. Back then he preferred profanity-ridden-angry-grunge-rock to anything that was remotely happy or peppy. How times had changed. For his kids, he was content to listen to the pop song of the day, whatever it was. He even found himself singing along sometimes. It was one of the lesser sacrifices he made.

Oh, how my teenage self would despise the man I have become, Robert thought. Two cars, two kids, a house, listening to pop music, losing my hair, slightly overweight, not famous, no longer trying to squeeze all the juice out of life. He could hear it now. I puke on your cookie cutter life you lousy middle-aged sellout, his teenage self would have said. Always so angry.

The radio played summer hit after summer hit, all of which Robert had heard almost daily for three months. During summer break, he had all but closed shop to stay with his kids. DSC he called it—short for Daddy's Summer Camp. It was cheaper than sending them to other camps. Business had been slow anyway. Or had it been slow because he had taken a break?

Chicken or the egg, Robert? Chicken or the egg?

While the kids sang along with Taylor Swift's hit of the summer—yes, he was listening to Taylor Swift, comparable to Brittney Spears of his era, although Taylor was arguably a better singer—Robert thought back to his session with Melissa Rodgers. His doubts were troubling. Had his brief interaction with Dr. Andersen skewed his worldview more than he realized? Was that all it took to rattle him? One session? One meditative experience?

He had to admit that it had been unusually deep—quasi-spiritual even. The meditation had unveiled the deepest sense of peace, of nothingness, that he had ever experienced.

What did that mean? Was his whole life a dream? Was the peace, the nothingness, the void, the only reality? Did this mean that he had to re-examine everything that he held true? Not only the way he conducted his therapy business, but his relationship to everything? Would that influence the way he interacted with his wife, his business, his kids!?

He had a great deal of difficulty contemplating that final thought. His kids were everything to him. Even thinking that their existence might be a dream as Dr. Andersen had suggested was too much for him.

No, this is real, he thought. Taylor Swift on the radio, driving in my car, shopping, cooking, brushing teeth, watching TV. This is reality. This. Here. Now.

Chapter 9

After the kids were in bed at 8.00 PM, Jessica and Robert sat down on their beige living room couch. Usually, they would watch an episode or two through their Netflix or Amazon Prime subscription, but tonight Jessica turned to Robert and wanted to know more about the events of the day.

"You've been quiet ever since you got home, Robert. What's going on? How did your consultation at the mental hospital go? Is everything okay?"

"I'm fine. Everything is fine," Robert replied, resisting the urge to spill his guts.

"That's crap and you know it Robert."

He didn't like it when she was so direct, confrontational even. If he were seeing himself and his wife as a couple in therapy, Robert would have reversed roles within the *Men are from Mars and Women are from Venus* paradigm, at least, when it came to emotional interactions. He was much more relational, i.e. feminine—probably why he was a therapist and the primary caretaker of the children—while she was much more direct and solution oriented, i.e. masculine. She wanted to know what was wrong and then she wanted to fix it.

"Something happened today," she continued, "I can see it. You're different, somehow."

He knew that look on her face. She wasn't going to give up.

"If I tell you, I would be breaking my confidentiality agreement," Robert answered reluctantly.

"Who would I tell? Come on Robert. We always talk about these things. Tell me what is going on."

Robert thought about it for a few seconds. He was dying to tell her, but he didn't know how she would react, didn't know if she would understand.

"My consultation today was with a suicidal patient," he finally blurted out.

"Suicidal? Robert. I went through all your studies with you. You're not qualified to consult with suicidal patients."

"Don't you think I know that?"

He paused.

"I was called in because of my meditation expertise."

"Your meditation expertise? Why?"

"Because the patient had been meditating for more than thirty years and they needed someone who had been meditating for more than twenty years to get him to talk."

"You haven't been meditating for twenty years."

"I know—but I did it, Jessica. I got him to talk by meditating with him, and, in the process, I experienced the deepest feeling of peace I have ever felt."

As he said that, Robert realized that the peace he had felt earlier was gone.

"When the patient began speaking," Robert continued, "he sounded unlike any person I have ever met before. Sure, his actions signaled that he was crazy, but his presence... Jessica, his presence was like what I imagine it would be to be close to a holy person or a spiritual master. I mean, that is really the only conclusion I can come to."

"And the holy guy tried to kill himself? Come on Robert. That just sounds ridiculous."

"Don't you think I know that? This is all I have been able to think about today. It's paradox. An oxymoron. A paramoron," he said, trying to lighten the mood with his signature wordplay. It was one of life's simple pleasures, even if it was juvenile, and it was rubbing off on his kids.

The other day he had coughed and laughed at the same time and his little girl had said: Dad, you're clauching, you know, coughing and laughing, clauching. That had made him claugh even harder.

Jessica didn't share their sense of word-based humor. Hers was more slapstick-oriented. She would laugh when Robert fell or knocked into something—not out of spite, she just couldn't control it.

The paramoron joke didn't get her to crack a smile. I should have said oxydox, he thought to himself. Humor always helped him. He had used it successfully as a child to diffuse many situations.

"Robert, I am worried about you. You took on a consulting job that we both know you are not qualified for and now you come home talking about this suicidal patient like he is some kind of a holy man. What's going on?"

"You're right. I never should have taken that job. It's just that…"

…I need my business work, I hate that you make more money than me, I am tired of being to cook and cleaner around the house, I saw this as an opportunity to change that, to turn my business into something more, plus, my interaction with Dr. Vigo Andersen was more intimate than any interaction with a human being for a long time…

"Just that what?" Jessica demanded.

"Nothing," Robert replied in resignation. "I was in over my head. This guy got to me. I promise that I will be back to my normal self by tomorrow. Okay?"

Jessica sighed in relief.

"Okay," she replied. "I am glad to hear that. You know that I support your therapy business Robert, but you have to stick with what you are good at—helping alcoholics and neurotic women. You're the relaxation guy, not the suicidal psychiatrist guy."

"Yeah, you're right," Robert replied. "I am the relaxation guy," he added with a smile.

Underneath, he knew that he wasn't going to be back to his normal self by tomorrow. He wanted to, but he wouldn't. Whatever had happened today had been profound, not something that Robert could resolve overnight. He would have to talk to someone about it, but not to her, not now. He was too confused. She was too demanding.

Jessica leaned in and they hugged.

"I just want you to be happy," she whispered in his ear.

"Me too," he replied.

They looked at each other.

"Are we okay?"

"We're okay."

"*NCIS?*"

"Sure."

They turned their attention from each other to the fifty-inch TV screen in their living room. It was a comforting distraction that had in many ways replaced the numbing effects of alcohol and tobacco in their lives. They were okay with that. Eating candy and watching TV had fewer side effects than drinking and smoking ever had.

Chapter 10

During his meditation session that night, Robert had a hard time calming his mind. He sat still, tried to focus his mind, and repeated his mantra.

One. One. One…

…but instead of deep peace, he experienced a vivid dialogue with his father—so vivid in fact, that he couldn't figure out if it was a memory from his childhood or a dream. It felt as if his father, the larger than life Brock Davis, were right there with him.

"Son," his father said, seemingly standing in their black and white eighties version of a kitchen, his signature crystal glass filled with cognac in hand, creating the symphony that Robert had fallen asleep to in his teens, ice cubes and crystal colliding, "this is a procreation planet."

It was evident that his father had been drinking, but he wasn't drunk. He had never been a fall-down-drunk when Robert was young, always kept his wits about him even if he drank almost every night. Now, Robert found himself sitting in the kitchen chair, feeling like a teenager, yet oddly grown up at the same time, and nodded.

"Masculine and feminine energies are always joining, creating something. You see, even when I am talking, my lips," Brock said, pointing to his lips while making sure that Robert saw that they were wet and round, "represent the feminine energy. My lips are being penetrated by the tongue," he said, sticking his tongue out and pointing to it, "which represents the masculine energy, creating the sounds you are hearing. This dualistic world we live in is always about the interaction between the masculine and feminine energies."

Robert remained muted, allowing his father to continue his monolog.

"We call it procreation, but it's really co-creation. The fertile Earth is feminine," Brock explained, drawing a big circle with his hand, "but it needs the masculine seeds," imitating sowing seeds with his fingers, "to grow," using his fist, pumping it up to his elbow through the imagined soil, probably in order to represent a tree, or something else uniquely masculine, Robert thought.

"If you take away the opposing play of masculine and feminine energies, you take away life, energy, passion, the ability to co-create," Robert's father continued.

"Men need women to be feminine if they want to be creative and women need men to be energetic, to seed them. This is the way the world has always worked son. It is not just biology; it is the nature of the universe. Without the interaction between these two energies, there would be no universe, no creation of any kind."

Brock paused, taking a sip of his cognac.

"That's why I think the feminist movement is dead wrong son. I understand their plea for equal rights, but what I hear these days — what you are being taught at school and by your mother — sounds like the preaching of sameness, not equality. What's going to happen to creation if everyone is the same? No sex, no passion, no creation — just asexual petri dish replication. And it's not just sex. You need the masculine and feminine energies to create ideas, and without ideas, there is no progress. By advocating sameness, androgyny, feminists today are putting a stop to evolution!" he finished by slamming the palm of his hand flat on the kitchen table, creating a loud bang — another staple in the Davis family late night symphony.

"Son, you need to understand this. Be a man. Embrace your masculine energy. Embrace your passion for life and your sexual energy. Be a creator, not a sexless robot."

Robert stared at this towering passionate man. To all others, he seemed to represent the pinnacle of success, the driven businessman, but to Robert, he was a failure in many ways, especially as a father. Yet, there he stood, sipping his cognac while preaching from a faltering pedestal about the one thing he was really good at.

"Robert Davis. Be a man."

It had been ten years since Robert's father had died, but when Robert opened his eyes after the evening's failed meditation attempt, he could have sworn that his father had been right there with him just a moment ago. The experience had been so realistic. Never before had he undergone such a strong dreamlike, no, lifelike experience during his time on the meditation cushions. Was it a memory, a dream, or something else? He couldn't tell.

Sitting still on the cushion for a moment, Robert thought about what his father's image had been saying about the interplay between masculine and feminine energies. Those ideas seemed to be far removed from his current reality. Was his father right? Had Robert sacrificed his creative sexual energy for family stability? Maybe to a degree, but his father's description of the situation was so black and white, so masculinely oriented. Maybe it represented a piece, but it sure as hell didn't paint the complete picture. Plus, being a man wasn't as straightforward a proposition today as it had been when Robert's father was in his prime. Being a man was… more complex.

Shake it off Robert, he thought. It was just your imagination, a hallucination. That conversation never took place. Let it go.

Yet, when he looked at Jessica—who was already asleep—his father's words, imagined or real, pointed to something of importance that Robert had been neglecting. The two of them were more like friends or partners these days, less like lovers. The interplay between masculine and feminine energies was almost non-existent.

Robert shook his head, stood up, stretched his legs, got into the king sized bed next to his wife, inserted his night guard over his teeth, turned off the nightlight on his bedside table, turned onto his left side, away from his wife, and closed his eyes. It had been a long, confusing day. He fell asleep knowing that he needed help.

Chapter 11

"Gentlemen. Robert asked me to call this special Council meeting on a Sunday night to discuss two huge topics. Meditation and death," Jack Miller announced.

Jack was a doctor of philosophy and Robert's best friend. The four of them, Robert, Jack, George, and the host, Arthur Thompson, had gathered in Arthur's living room. He was the oldest in the group, at sixty-two, while the other three were in their mid-forties. Arthur was a widower who had lost his wife to cancer in his early fifties, and because he lived alone, he had offered to host this special meeting. Arthur's living room was filled with a strange combination of Native American spiritual artifacts, Buddha statues, and family pictures. Each of the men sat in a comfy, upholstered, oak, dining room chair, forming a circle.

The Council, as they called themselves, was Robert's creation. He had congregated the four of them from different facets of his life because he no longer felt adequately stimulated by the twelve step meetings he regularly attended. Unlike emotional support groups, the Council was meant to be a group for deep philosophical and spiritual conversations. After a period of three years, their gatherings had become indispensable to each of the men involved. Through their conversations, intense debates, and occasional arguments, they had created a strong bond. The Council met once or twice every month, usually for late dinner in the back room at Kerbey Lane Cafe in North West Austin, but this meeting demanded more time and no disturbance from the outside world.

Tonight they had begun with a short moment of silence, suggested by Arthur, who'd said: We can't begin before we arrive. Before that, he had doused them with a smoking bundle of Sage incense, explaining that it was meant to cleanse their aura. Arthur always brought a unique and deeply spiritual perspective to the group, but sometimes his New Agey rhetoric made Robert cringe. This time, however, the silence was welcome and the Sage provided a pleasant aroma. The combination gave the group a moment to synchronize their energies before the discussion began.

"Robert? You want to get the conversation rolling? Frame the discussion?" Jack said after the initial ceremonies had been completed.

"Yeah, sure," Robert answered. "First, let me thank you all for coming on such short notice, and, special thanks to you Arthur, for hosting this. I don't think Kerbey Lane would have created the right atmosphere for our discussion."

He took care to look around and acknowledge each of the men as he spoke.

"Five days ago, I had what I would characterize as the most inexplicable experience of my life," he continued. "Unfortunately, I can't tell you, gentlemen, all the details—so please don't ask—but the experience involved meditation and death, a strange combination to say the least. In all honesty, the event unnerved me. Since I can't speak to anyone about it—not in the way that I want to anyway—I thought that the next best thing would be to talk to you guys, to get your perspective on these two topics. I would like to know how and if you meditate and what that means to you, and furthermore, to hear about how you relate to death. In my mind, these two topics weren't related at all until last week, so maybe it's best to talk about them separately, talk about meditation first and then death, or vice versa."

"Sure," Jack responded. He was the natural facilitator for their group discussions because of his philosophy training. "I second the idea and suggest that we start with meditation and then talk about death. Who wants to get the ball rolling?"

"I'll do it," answered George Martinez. "I mean, I don't meditate much. I know some breathing techniques that I use when I am stressed, and I pray rather frequently. That's like meditation, right?"

Sometimes Robert didn't know why he had brought George into the group. He was a five-foot-two Latino insurance salesman in his mid-forties that Robert had met at one of the networking events he frequented in Austin. They had started talking, found out that they had kids at a similar age and then met several times over coffee. Their conversations were always existential in nature, about the meaning of life, meditation, and philosophy, but when Robert thought back to their interactions, he realized that he had done most of the talking, not George. He was a nice enough guy, easy to talk to—probably why he was such a good salesman—but the truth was that seldom, if ever, did George contribute significantly to a group discussion.

"They say that prayer is talking to God while meditation is listening to God," Arthur said in his deep, resonant voice.

Of course he has to bring God into the equation, Robert thought, admitting to himself that even this somewhat regurgitated wisdom sounded profound when Arthur said it. What he would give to have such a rich voice.

"Then I must be doing most of the talking because I hardly ever sit still and listen. I know you guys do it, and we've often talked about that, but, I mean, I don't have the time," George replied. "When do you guys find the time?"

"I practice in the evening," Robert replied, worried that this meeting would turn into a meditation training session rather than a conversation between equals.

"I sit every morning and every evening for twenty minutes," Arthur said.

"You see, I don't have that kind of extra time," George replied.

"I practice on occasion," Jack interjected, "sometimes three times a week, sometimes every day, sometimes once a month, sometimes in the morning, sometimes in the evening. I'd like to make it a regular part of my life, but, I don't know, I guess I just practice when I really need it."

Robert recognized that Arthur was the only real meditator in the room, the only one who could possibly shed light on what Dr. Andersen was going through.

"Can you share your secret Arthur? Tell us why you meditate so consistently?" Jack asked, stealing the words right out of the Robert's mouth.

"Well, I think of it as my communion with God," Arthur answered.

God again, Robert thought to himself. What if a person doesn't believe in God? He wanted to ask the question but knew it would likely open up a can of worms, creating yet another topic of discussion.

"I begin every session with a prayer. Then I sit completely still and envision the light and love of God enveloping me," Arthur continued. "It is the most blessed time of the day for me. I would rather miss meals than miss my meditation routine."

"I thought that meditation was about emptying the mind," George interrupted.

That's why I like having him around, Robert thought. He always asks the questions that I wish I would have the guts to ask. I don't want to reveal my ignorance, but he is fine with not knowing. He doesn't pretend.

"Well," Arthur answered, "I don't believe there is such a thing as emptiness. In this world, there is either light or dark. Nothing is empty. That's why I attract light during my meditation, I make space for it."

No such thing as emptiness!?

"How then would you explain the forty plus minutes of absolute silence, peace—I would dare say emptiness—that I experienced earlier this week?" Robert blurted out.

"Well... " Arthur paused for a moment and then shifted in his chair. "You say that the emptiness you experienced was peaceful, correct?"

"Yes."

"Then I would respond by saying that it wasn't really emptiness. I would say that there wasn't nothing. There was peace, and to me, peace is light," Arthur explained, taking his time, pronouncing each word with care.

"That could be one way of interpreting it," Robert replied, "but the peace didn't feel like light or anything else really. It was just deep, empty, peaceful."

"If I may," Jack said, elbowing his way into the disagreement between Arthur and Robert, "it sounds like the two of you are talking about the difference between duality and nonduality."

Jack often did that, sat back and then brought in a philosophical perspective that wasn't immediately visible to the rest of them.

"Arthur," Jack continued, "by contrasting light and dark, you are speaking of duality, of opposites, right? And Robert, as I understand it, you are referring to the philosophical concept of nonduality, often described by practitioners as emptiness—a concept synonymous with Eastern mysticism."

Early in his career, Jack had focused exclusively on Western philosophy, but in recent years, he had begun to study Eastern philosophy and mysticism. He had even published several articles comparing the works of the masters, such as Plato and Aristotle, to philosophies that originated in the East. There were commonalities, but not as many as Jack had wished to find. Yet, his interest in the subject remained undeterred.

Robert thought about Jack's diagnosis. The Zen monks he'd studied with had told Robert to let go of everything. They had likened meditation to deep, dreamless sleep while awake, or alternately described it as the eye in the center of the storm. His moments of peace were exactly that, peaceful, empty, deep. That sense had only deepened when he had his experience with Dr. Andersen earlier in the week—but Arthur didn't agree.

"One of my teachers repeatedly said that the concept of emptiness was theoretically invalid, that there was no such thing as emptiness or nonduality, that when an emptiness occurred in the universe, the void was immediately filled with either light or darkness," Arthur countered.

What Robert would give to have such a commanding voice, such presence. By the mere force of his voice, Arthur made everything sound believable.

"Emptiness or light, what difference does it make," George chimed in, "for people like me who have a hard time relaxing?"

"From what I understand, it has to do with stages of meditation," Jack explained, happy to be able to share his academic knowledge of the subject. "People begin with learning how to relax, then they learn how to concentrate or visualize, and then, at later stages, and with proper guidance, they enter the nondual state, often referred to as emptiness."

Robert concurred. It was the process that he taught at his meditation workshops, except that he didn't spend a lot of time on teaching visualization. To him, it was a waste of time.

"With all due respect, to both you and Robert, I have been meditating consistently for longer than all three of you put together. I can tell you, without a doubt, both from my own experience and from the experience of my teachers, that focusing on emptiness creates a vacuum for energies that you don't want to attract," Arthur said, adamantly defending his position.

This was one of the things that Robert loved about meeting this group. The diversity of opinions always encouraged him to examine a topic from more than one perspective. When they'd first met, they had agreed that they were meeting to challenge each other, not to nod their heads in complacency like a choir responding to a preacher's sermon. As a result, Robert had always left their meetings feeling mentally richer than when he'd arrived, even when he disagreed vehemently with what was being said, as was now the case. Their commitment to being friends first—no matter what was said at the meetings—was such that Robert felt secure in pursuing his point, as he staunchly disagreed with Arthur.

"Okay, Arthur. We know that you have been meditating for the longest time, but you approach the practice from a New Age perspective. You are always talking about God and some external energies that you are either attracting or synchronizing with. I have been meditating off and on for twenty years, consistently for five, and I have not experienced any of what you are talking about. I go into my peaceful state and it feels empty. Not once have I met God, and not once has my mind been filled with darkness," Robert said, working up to his final point. "Isn't this light you talk about just part of your imagination? Aren't you simply projecting all the ideas that you have picked up over the years in a kind of self-fulfilling prophecy?"

Robert made an effort to sound polite. He sincerely respected Arthur—part of him even saw Arthur as a father figure—but all too often, Arthur's New Age concepts were way outside of Robert's rational worldview, plus, they usually did not rhyme with his personal experiences.

Arthur smiled and replied: "Point taken brother, but wasn't it Albert Einstein who said that imagination was more important than intelligence?"

Oh, no, Robert thought to himself. Derailing a good point about his own mental projections by quoting Einstein? Man, this guy has a response to everything. And calling me brother while we disagree, both patronizing and a sign of goodwill at the same time. How do I respond?

George, who was the people-person in the room, and probably highly codependent, picked up on the tension and said: "Well, once more, we have to agree to disagree."

Jack added: "Yes, but this is a fascinating conflict nonetheless. The two of you say that you are both engaged in the same practice, yet you have wildly different approaches and outcomes. And there doesn't seem to be a way to resolve the issue because the practice is completely internal. How do we know which one of you is telling the truth when both of you believe that what you are saying is true?"

Yes, that was the central dilemma, wasn't it? How to distinguish truth from what people believed to be true?

Dr. Andersen, for example, was completely convinced that emptiness was not only real but that it superseded the human condition as ultimate reality.

Arthur was convinced that his dualistic visualization process was the way to go, focusing on the light while keeping the darkness at bay, probably based on deeply instilled concepts of good and evil from when he was a child. He had been raised in a strict religious Baptist environment, which he had turned away from in his early twenties. He had found religion again in his forties through a Unity church, which was a New Age institution if there ever was one. Good and evil, light and darkness. That was Arthur's premise.

And himself? Well, Robert wasn't convinced of anything. He had tried not to approach meditation from a philosophical or religious standpoint but had rather wanted to learn the mechanics, the techniques to create moments of peace, to hit the reset button when his emotions were getting the better of him. He'd wanted to replace the need for numbing—which he had previously done with drugs and alcohol—with something that had fewer unpleasant side effects. For him, it had worked, at least, so far.

"There is no way to know, is there?" Robert said while looking at Arthur.

"Yes, there is. Over the years, I have learned to trust my experiences rather than dogma and philosophy," Arthur answered, "and my experiences tell me that nothing is empty, that voids are always filled with something."

"Yet, it is also evident, that your firsthand experiences are colored by your philosophy, by your approach," Jack quickly added, never afraid of stating the obvious when he noticed it.

"Brother Jack," Arthur replied. "You asked me why I sat, why I meditated, and I answered. I am attracted to bathing myself in the light. You, on the other hand, are book-wise when it comes to this subject, much more so than I, but you have very little experience with meditation, as you confessed. I think that, in this instance, experience trumps knowledge. Yes? At least, I am at peace, even as I am getting older, even after I have lost my wife to cancer. I am at peace, thanks to meditation, thanks to being in the light."

The room fell silent. What else was there to say? They could continue debating, but it was evident that the novice George, the book-wise Jack, the skeptic practitioner Robert, and the mystic Arthur, had all made their case, had shared their points of view, and, as had happened so many times before, were at an impasse. Despite that, they all smiled because they enjoyed the process of exchanging ideas without necessarily coming to a conclusion.

Of course, it was the codependent George who broke the silence. "Well, that was interesting. I think I need a bathroom break before we start talking about death," he said in a comical voice.

The room exploded in laughter.

"Yes, bathroom break and ice tea," Arthur replied as they stood up. "I thought we could take the rest of the meeting outside. It's such a beautiful night and I have the fire pit ready in the backyard."

Chapter 12

It was a perfect starlit Texas autumn evening, cloudless with temperatures in the mid-seventies. Arthur's house was situated on the east side of Round Rock, a small town just north of Austin. His spacious yard was up against an open, undeveloped area, so there was zero light pollution, making an infinite number of stars visible to the naked eye. In the yard, Arthur had built a sizeable fire, much larger than anything Robert could ever burn in his backyard chiminea.

The transition from the living room, including the lighting of the fire, had taken a little more than thirty minutes. Now, with the light turned off on the patio, the four men sat together, each in a lawn chair of their own on the house side of the fire pit, switching their attention between the stars and the fire, enveloped in a cocoon of darkness, the light from the flames dancing on their faces. The crackle and pop of the fire were the only sounds that they could hear.

"Imagine," Jack said, breaking the silence. "Each one of the tiny specks of lights we are seeing is a sun, the same as the one in our solar system. There isn't a human alive who can look at the night sky and say, I understand. None of us understand the infinite universe. Most people who start thinking about it, get overwhelmed, shrug their shoulders, and turn their attention back to something mundane, like drinking beer or watching TV. Only a few great minds have ever actually contemplated the nature of the universe. Fewer still have done it without going insane. The same holds true in regards to smaller mysteries, like the psychological and spiritual nature of man, or biological diversity. Only a few great minds have begun to tackle the difficult questions of life and death."

There was a short pause.

"I wish I were one of them," Jack said, with pure longing in his voice, "but in my study of philosophy over the years, I have felt dwarfed by the great minds and their ability to philosophize. Dwarfed, I tell you, just like I feel now, looking at the night sky."

It was one of many philosophical monologs that the group had heard Jack deliver, but this one was different. They had never heard him confess to what was effectively an intellectual inferiority complex. It was difficult for the others to hear—as he was the smartest one in the group by far—yet, no one responded. It was one of the few rules the Council had. They weren't meeting to fix each other. If one of the men wanted to express himself, he was free to do so in a safe space without fearing judgment. Only when someone asked for advice were members of the group allowed to give it to him and Jack had not asked for any. The others simply let him express himself and remained silent.

Robert was mesmerized by the fire. A part of him wished that he could light a fire every night. He'd rather do that than watch an episode or two of some TV series that wouldn't influence his life in one way or another, except by providing him with a temporary distraction. But, his wife wasn't into sitting by the fire. Too hot. Too many bugs, she would say, and because Robert didn't want to sacrifice time with her, lighting a fire at the Davis home was only done on rare occasions.

This moment, however, was perfect. Four guys sitting in the silence. The fire was alive. Prancing. Flickering. Beguiling. Hypnotizing. Robert felt a deep sense of peace wash over him.

"So guys, are we going to talk about death now? I have to head home in about thirty minutes," George finally declared, breaking the silence. "I need to get up early in the morning. Big meeting, you know."

As if snapped out of a trance the other guys sat up rather hastily.

"Yes, of course," Arthur replied. "The time just got away from us, didn't it?"

"Yeah… yeah, it did," Jack added, responding to his role as the supposed facilitator of this special meeting. "Robert, again, this is pretty much up to you. You still want to talk about death?"

"I guess, I mean if you guys don't mind. I know we don't have much time, but if you could just briefly share your experiences and your ideas about what happens, that would be very helpful," Robert replied.

"Why don't you go first?" Arthur asked, looking at Robert.

"Okay. Ah, to me death has always been hidden, a total mystery. I don't see death in my line of work. In fact, I confess to you gentlemen, that, at forty-five, I have only seen two dead bodies in my life, my father and my grandmother. But now, as I enter my midlife, I think about it more, you know, what it is and what will happen—if anything. In my youth I pretty much ascribed to a Godless philosophy, that death was the end of it all... "

Robert looked deeply into the fire.

"...but death can't be the final word, can it? I mean, look at this fire. The wood that we threw on it has been decimated, or so it seems, but in reality, the wood has been transformed into gasses and ashes. I think about that, you know, about how nothing is ever destroyed, but only changes form. When it comes to human beings, I don't know if the personality lives on when a person dies, but something lives on, just in a different form, right? Does that make any sense? I mean, do you guys believe that death is it or do you believe there is something more?"

"All I know about death is what the Bible tells me," George said.

The men knew that George went to Catholic mass with his wife and rather sizeable extended family every Sunday, and to underline his Catholicism, he continually joked about only having five kids.

"The Bible says that if I live a good life, then I go to Heaven, but if I sin, then I go to Hell."

George paused, seemingly thinking about whether or not to go on.

"I don't know if I believe that. A part of me wants to—it is my heritage after all—but our talks over the past three years have made me rethink several things, death being one of them. I haven't come to any new conclusion. In a way, I am like you Robert. I haven't seen many dead bodies or experienced much death in my life."

"That's the problem, isn't it? Our youth enamored society hides death from us, makes us believe that we will live forever," Jack asserted, rather forcefully. "We don't want to see death. We even hide old people so that we don't have to be reminded of our own mortality. In other cultures, old age is celebrated, embraced even. Death is a part of life. Monks in several Eastern traditions work with dead bodies to remind themselves of the transient nature of the world. Some yogis smear themselves with ashes from funeral pyres for the same purpose, to remember that life is fragile. But we, in the West, have inoculated ourselves against death by putting on blinders, pretending that we don't have to face it, yet underneath, we are scared, fearful, anxious. Maybe that's because we have denied the existence of the single biggest mystery in life."

"Wow Jack," Robert replied, reacting to his friend's emotional delivery. "Why don't you tell us how you really feel?"

"It just really bugs me," Jack retorted. "There is not a single person I have met in my lifetime who is comfortable talking about death. It's the biggest downside to our youth-centric culture. Death is a bummer, so let's not talk about it. Let's hide it away and hope it never strikes close to home."

"What about people who believe that it is somehow possible to prepare for death or even instigate it through meditation?" Robert said, trying to sneak in the real question that was on his mind. "What about people who begin to think that the meditative state, however it manifests itself, is more real than life itself, and then equate that state with everlasting life?"

"I've read about that," Jack responded, "about yogis especially, who have reportedly transitioned willingly from life to death while meditating. There is a chapter at the end of *An Autobiography of a Yogi* that claims that Paramahansa Yogananda made his transition this way. The publishers referred to some scientific evidence about how long it took for his body to begin to deteriorate to back their claim up."

Robert had heard that before. That book had been on his reading list for a while, but he had not gotten to it. He did notice, however, that the way Jack spoke about transitioning sounded an awful lot like what Dr. Andersen had been saying.

"So what do you think?" Robert asked Jack. "Is there any truth to these claims?"

"I don't know," Jack replied. "As far as I am concerned, they are unsubstantiated theories. At the same time, there seem to be an awful lot of them floating around in Eastern mysticism. Every other form of mythology has some sort of life after death scenario, but Eastern concepts are more sophisticated than agrarian myths from the same time period, which makes some philosophers take them more seriously. This aspect, though, the ability to die willfully, consciously, I doubt it. It's not happening anywhere in the world today, not as far as I know. If the practice could be passed on, and people were still doing it, then I think that we would see some reporting on it. Personally, I think it's just another type of mythology, however sophisticated it may seem."

"Brothers," Arthur's deep voice interrupted, pulling their attention directly to him. "Regretfully, I have had plenty of experience with death, more than I care for. I have lost both my parents, two of my siblings, several friends, and my wife. All I can say is this. Death is the great mystery, one that I entrust to God. I have read all the books, listened to spiritual teacher after spiritual teacher tell me about theories of death—some of which have been quite interesting—but when it comes down to it, when death is faced, philosophies and explanations fade away, as consoling as they may be. Experiencing death firsthand is scary and liberating at the same time. It is both, mysterious and mundane. Death can be simultaneously joyous and sad, as it was in the case of my wife. Joyous, because she was released from immense pain. Sad, because I miss her dearly every single day. Yet, I have found that my grief has become a consoling partner rather than a source of pain. I don't know if meditation and death are connected in some way—they don't seem to be. All I can tell you is that through the practice of meditation, which for me is like showering in light, I have discovered peace that has allowed me to transform sadness into joyous memories. In my mind, that is the only connection there is between death and meditation."

There was complete silence as the men allowed what Arthur had said to sink in. Death can be joyous and sad. Grief is a consoling partner. Coupled with his experiences, Arthur's words carried weight.

The firewood had been unusually dry and the fire had burned fast and furiously. The flames were dying down and the stars were more visible than before. The darkness seemed to be moving in from all sides, underscoring the absolute silence.

Yes, Robert thought. Death is the great mystery.

Then, when no one had spoken for approximately two minutes, George said: "I'm sorry guys, but I really have to go."

"Yes, yes, of course," Robert replied. "I am not sure that we could have ended the conversation any better than this. Thank you for coming on such short notice, my brothers. Your ideas were very helpful."

Within ten minutes the chairs had been folded and put away, the men had said their goodbyes, and in the yard, all that was left were the smoldering embers of the fire.

Chapter 13

It was a little after midnight when Robert got home and he was wide awake. As he walked into his house, he sensed that everyone was already sleeping—as they should be—except for the dog, Sandy, who greeted him at the door. He drank a glass of water, turned off the lights in the kitchen, and walked to the other end of the house.

Entering the master bedroom, he saw that Jessica had left his bedside table light on. He felt a slight pang of guilt in his stomach because he assumed that the light bothered her as it would him, even though she had repeatedly told him that she loved falling asleep with the light on, said that she enjoyed drifting off to him either reading or meditating, said that it felt comforting.

He stopped for a moment and looked at Jessica in the same way that he had gazed deeply into the fire earlier that evening. She was still beautiful, with her blonde hair, distinct features, and attractive lips. He adored it when she smiled. Yet, as he stood there, Robert didn't feel the same kind of tug on his heartstrings as he had felt when they first started dating. His love for her was less passionate, yet somehow more significant and enduring.

They had met in Seattle fifteen years ago and moved around quite a bit, especially during their first five years together, before they settled in Austin when she got pregnant. Even during those years of gypsy-like living, all he needed was to look at her and he knew that he was home.

That was how he felt now. At home. Comforted. Like he belonged. Was that his new definition of love? Passion replaced with a profound sense of connection?

As he watched her sleeping—experiencing the warmth in his heart—Robert noticed that Jessica's face was less peaceful than it had been in years past. The sides of her mouth were turned down and her eyes were heavy. It looked like she had been knocked out rather than as she were enjoying a peaceful rest. He knew that she was working hard and never took time to herself, never unwound her nerves in the same way that he did through relaxation and meditation. He had encouraged her to do so a few times, told her to make time for herself, but she didn't listen to him, not like his clients did. Of course, she wasn't supposed to—he wasn't her therapist and didn't want to be—but sometimes he wished that she would listen, at least partially. Now, Robert felt guilty for placing the burden of providing for the family almost solely on her. He needed to step up his game, both as an earner and as a husband. She deserved better.

Facing the well-lit mirror above the two sink vanity, Robert looked intently at his own face while brushing his teeth. His receding hairline was higher on his head than last time he looked and his goatee was approximately seventy percent gray. The other day, his daughter had told him that he looked like a grandpa—not very encouraging. Gray or not, his goatee did a good job of hiding his double chin, which was why he had it in the first place. All in all, the physical changes brought on by age weren't doing him any favors. Then again, neither was his lifestyle of high candy intake, all too frequent takeaway meals, and low levels of exercise. The mirror did not give him any illusions of immortality.

Age. Mortality.

In recent years, Robert had become increasingly sensitive to his own inevitable death. He knew that it was because he was entering midlife and walked into it with open eyes. Yet, he was feeling the effects just as much as everyone else. He could not escape it. Midlife was a time of reflection. For the past twenty years, everything had been about somehow getting better; rebuilding after realizing he was an alcoholic, finding a mate, starting a family, getting a degree, building a business. Now, his future in the therapy business didn't look as bright as it used to, his kids needed him less and less, and his wife was entirely independent of him, opposite to when they first met. He occasionally felt like no one would miss him if he vanished off the face of the earth.

I guess I understand why people contemplate suicide, he thought. If I, in my rather fortunate situation, am wondering what to live for, I can just imagine what people in truly unfortunate circumstances allow themselves to contemplate.

He had seriously thought about committing suicide once in his life, while drunk in his late teens, sitting on the top of a cliff while on a camping trip with some friends, supposedly living the healthy life but, in reality, drinking and fornicating. While he sat there on the edge, drunk as he was, he realized two things. First, he didn't have the guts to go through with it, and second, he was curious about what life had to offer. He had wondered if it could get better.

Looking in the mirror now, nearly thirty years later, he knew that he still didn't have the guts—not that he was considering suicide—but, at the same time, he was less curious about life, more jaded. Sure, he loved helping his clients, when he could, but there weren't that many of them anymore. Business had been slowing down. What really kept him focused on living were his children, James and Cathy, the two suns around which his solar system revolved.

Was that what Dr. Vigo Andersen lacked? Robert thought. A reason to live? He had no family. Few clients. No community that he belonged to. If Robert could entertain thoughts about his premature departure with all that he had, then why not Dr. Andersen? But it didn't compute. It just didn't. Deep peace had emanated from that man—the deepest sense of peace Robert had ever felt. Maybe Dr. Andersen's problem wasn't community or lack thereof. Maybe it was philosophy. He sincerely believed that ultimate reality was found only in the meditative state. Can the meditative state really be so interpretive? Robert wondered.

In all the studies that he had seen, the physiological effects of meditation always seemed to be the same—same kinds of brainwave states and same kinds of relaxing hormones. That effectively meant that everyone was experiencing something similar. Yet, people's interpretations of their meditative experiences varied greatly. Could philosophy really matter as much as technique?

All of this went through Robert's mind as he was getting ready for bed. He checked in on the kids, who were soundly asleep, turned on the security system, and set his alarm for 6 AM in the morning. As he sat on the edge of his bed, he noticed that the time was now 12.40 AM. He looked at his two blankets and meditation cushion. He knew he didn't have time, knew that he needed to get up early to get his kids ready for school, but his mind was racing in a thousand different directions. He wasn't about to fall asleep anytime soon. So, instead of crawling under the thin summer covers with his mind in overdrive, he heeded the call of his meditation corner and sat.

One. One. One. One.

Slower.

One. One. One.

With the breath.

One. One.

Emptiness.

But something wasn't right. The emptiness, which was usually so peaceful, felt unfamiliar somehow. Robert's body shuddered when he opened his eyes after only ten minutes of sitting. He stood up, tried to shake off the uneasy feeling, and went to bed, hoping that this had just been a one-time occurrence. He couldn't afford to lose his meditation practice, not now. He needed his reset button to work.

Chapter 14

With a small cup of coffee in hand, Robert leafed through magazines at Starbucks inside a two-story upper-class Barnes & Noble in the Arboretum while munching on a lemon pound cake and drinking a large cup of coffee. Breakfast of champions. No wonder the mirror wasn't his best friend.

In between sips, Robert yawned. It had taken a herculean effort for him to wake up that Monday morning. He usually looked forward to starting the workweek, but his late night soiree with the Council had taken a toll. He had only slept four hours, which was not nearly enough. In fact, it was the exact opposite of what he preached to his kids and clients.

Robert's lack of sleep wasn't the only thing bothering him. He was sincerely worried about the decline of his therapy business. There weren't enough new clients coming in. He knew that he ought to be doing something to market his business instead of leafing through magazines, but, at the same time, he felt exhausted by the incessant promotion that needed to be done. He was fed up with the social media efforts, the networking events, the blogs, and the email blasts that were meant to pick up business. He felt like two voices were ceaselessly battling inside his head.

One said: Market, market, market!

The other said: Take it easy. Social media isn't working for you. It's word of mouth that counts.

It was hard to be a solopreneur, especially when tireless efforts weren't rewarded. That was why, today, instead of doing a million things and then being disappointed when none of them worked, Robert made an effort to muffle the marketing voice that was nagging him and did none of what he was supposed to be doing. It was becoming an uncomfortable pattern.

People are just damn good at ignoring things, he had told a colleague while discussing marketing efforts two weeks ago. I mean, I know that I am. I ignore more information than I process. It's hard not to do, with ceaseless stimuli attacking you from all directions. How do you market yourself in a world where everyone is an expert at ignoring everyone else?

His colleague didn't know the answer to that question, nor did Robert, which was why he did nothing now—part inertia, part helplessness.

"Robert?"

His reverie was interrupted by a familiar voice and a distinct smell of Old Spice cologne. Robert looked up. It was George Martinez, wearing his insurance salesman warrior outfit—white shirt, blue tie, and dress pants, his black hair slicked back, his face newly shaven. He looked and smelled fresh, unlike Robert, who hadn't bothered to freshen up earlier that morning—the weekend's stubble still surrounded his goatee and he hadn't showered.

"What are you doing here?" George asked.

"I'm waiting. I don't have a client until later in the morning," Robert answered, feeling like he had been caught skipping school.

"I had an early meeting at 7 AM this morning and I am meeting a client here at 10 AM. Do you mind if I sit with you until he arrives?"

"No, no, of course not. Be my guest," Robert answered while tidying up the table, stacking the magazines, setting the plate with the cake crumbs aside, and picking up his coffee cup to make room.

"Man, that was some meeting last night," George said as he sat down. "Totally blew my mind. I didn't fall asleep until 1.30 or 2 AM."

Really? Robert responded internally. Considering your input, it didn't seem like you enjoyed it at all. You really enjoyed it, huh, he kept thinking. You keep surprising me.

Of course, Robert didn't say that—rather he responded: "Yes, that was some meeting. I had trouble sleeping as well. What did you think about that kept you awake?"

"What wasn't I thinking about?" George replied with a question, shaking his head while his hair stayed in place thanks to copious amounts of product.

"My mind was all over the place," he continued, "but, you know, when I couldn't sleep I tried meditating like Arthur described it; first praying, then sitting still, imagining myself being bathed in light. I didn't feel much, but I guess it takes practice, huh?"

Naturally he would try Arthur's approach, being a Catholic and all, Robert thought.

"Yes, it takes practice," Robert responded.

"I also thought about what you said, about the stick of wood thrown onto the flames, how it doesn't get destroyed but is rather transformed into ashes and gasses. That was deep," George added.

"That's not my idea to begin with," Robert replied, "but I find it strangely comforting."

George nodded.

"You know that I don't believe in God, right? Not in that same way that you and Arthur do," Robert said.

"Yes, of course, I know that. It's not exactly a secret," George replied.

"Not that I am an atheist," Robert continued. "I am more like an agnostic. I just don't know what to believe exactly. I keep thinking that there has to be some underlying organizing principle. Thinking of death like a stick thrown onto a fire—the elements returned to the great unknown—helps me deal with the idea of my own mortality."

They both took a sip of their coffee.

"You know Robert, I realize that I didn't say much last night, that I don't always express myself," George said, "but I feel like such a novice compared to you, Jack, and especially Arthur."

"Arthur does have that way about him, doesn't he?" Robert responded.

"Yes," George replied, and smiled awkwardly, "but, I was really interested in listening to you guys. You brought up things that I had never thought about. I don't really meditate, so your descriptions were eye opening, and when it came to speaking about death, well, as

I said last night, I really don't have much experience. I was blown away by Arthur's description of how meditating on the light helped console him through times of grief. I couldn't stop thinking about it on my way home."

"Yes, Arthur had quite the impact," Robert answered, remembering how the tension between him and Arthur had been palpable for a period of time last night, even though they had said their goodbyes with a warm embrace.

"Jack made some excellent points as well, don't you think, about the stages of meditation and different perspectives on death between cultures, especially about how we tend to hide mortality in our society," Robert added.

"I guess," George responded, "but I find that Jack is sometimes too intellectual," he added. "I often have a hard time following exactly what he means."

Interesting, Robert thought.

He held exactly the opposite view, that George and especially Arthur, were too emotional, which was doubtlessly how Jessica felt about him sometimes.

"Well, that's probably why we meet," Robert replied, "you know, to expand our horizons, see the world from each other's perspectives, right?" he asked himself, as much as he was asking George.

"Yes, exactly," George said enthusiastically, "and Robert, let me just thank you one more time for letting me be a part of the group. It means the world to me."

Robert looked at George's smiling face and sincere eyes. To his surprise, he saw that George really meant what he was saying. Maybe it wasn't always about the man contributing to the group, Robert thought. Sometimes it was about the group contributing to the man.

Robert smiled. The encounter with George had lifted him out of thoughts of self-pity and irritation. He was genuinely glad that the insurance salesman was a part of the Council.

Chapter 15

"He's just so angry all the time Mr. Davis."

Robert's only client that day was Mildred Wallace, a nice looking, lean, white-haired woman in her early seventies—a cut out from the TV show *Golden Girls* if there ever was one. She was talking about her husband Joe of fifty years.

"He just sits in his chair watchin' Fox News half the day and then yells at me and the kids—when they come visit, which they rarely do anymore—about how this country is going to hell, how we must reclaim America's greatness, how gay liberals are ruining the moral fiber of society, how the government is coming for our guns, about Benghazi or some other scandal of the day. I've been married to the man for fifty years and I've always known he was a conservative. That never bothered me, but he has changed, I'm tellin' you. These days he is just so damned angry all the time, and when I say somethin', he blames me, tells me that I was too liberal when raisin' our kids. I just can't handle all this anger, Mr. Davis. What should I do?"

Mildred or Millie, as she insisted Robert call her—even though she wouldn't speak of calling him anything except Mr. Davis—wasn't the first woman who came to him crying about this problem. Justified anger was all the rage, Robert thought to himself, amused by his own pun. But it wasn't just conservatives. He had plenty of liberal friends who spent their free time being outraged on Facebook, publicly shaming anyone who wasn't PC enough—so much so that he had stopped following many of them, even unfriended a few, whatever that meant.

"Well, Millie, I am sympathetic to your situation" Robert replied, trying not to yawn. "No one should have to endure so much anger in their surroundings. However, I need to clarify. Are you asking me to help you fix Joe, or, are you asking me how to live with Joe?"

"I was hopin' we could do somethin' to soften him up," Mildred answered. "We are old people now Mr. Davis. I don't expect that we will be gettin' a divorce at this point. Maybe a combination of both, a little bit of fixin' and a little bit of learnin' how to cope," she added with a hopeful smile.

"That was what I was afraid of," Robert said. "I can't help you when it comes to fixing Joe. Only Joe can stop Joe from being angry. It seems to me that he has found justification for expressing his anger, seeing as so many people do it on TV all the time, but it is his anger. He is angry, for whatever reason, and only he can change that. I must tell you, though, in my experience, most people don't change until they absolutely have to. They don't change until their behavior becomes too painful to tolerate."

Robert thought about how that continued to be the case in his personal situation. Change only happened when his behavior became too painful. Robert wanted it to be different. With all his experience and information, he ought to be able to change sooner; ought to be able to respond to the shadow of the whip instead of responding to the pain of the lashing. He was working on it.

"But it's already too painful for me Mr. Davis," Mildred replied. "That's why I am here."

"Yes, I understand that Millie, but Joe is not here is he?"

"No."

"And why not? Did you invite him to come with you?"

"Yes, but he wouldn't have it. Said that I was the one with the problem."

"Exactly. He does not see his behavior as a problem. Therefore, he will not change."

Mildred looked deflated. Her eyes lost what little gleam of hope she'd had when she'd entered Robert's office.

"What do I do?" she asked, "I am at the end of my rope."

"I can't tell you precisely what to do Millie," Robert replied, wishing that he could take away her pain—like when he hugged his children after they fell and told them that everything was going to be alright—but that wasn't how the therapy business worked. "All I can

Chapter 17

All too often friendship was about proximity. When Robert had quit drinking, he had consciously decided that he would choose his friends from that point forward. Stick to the winners, he was told. But as he moved around the country, he realized that beggars can't be choosers. More often than not you settle for who is in your proximity or you have no friends at all. Because he excluded heavy drinkers, as a rule, this meant that Robert had often been without friends in the past.

Understanding this made him appreciate his five-year friendship with Jack Miller all the more. In addition to meeting with the Council, Jack and Robert met every other week for coffee or a midday snack. Jack taught philosophy and controlled his own time outside of classes and because Robert had fewer clients than he wanted to, they were able to meet during the day while other people worked. This saved them from any clashes with scheduled family time.

"Did you know that most of the great philosophers didn't have a family?" Jack exclaimed, sitting in a deep orange armchair in the corner of a tiny local coffee house a few blocks from where Robert lived. His lanky legs were cramped for space, his dark hair unkempt, his pointy nose and chin angling slightly away from Robert.

"I understand why," Jack continued, "I mean, I have no time to think. All I do is deal with flippant and disinterested students all day, take care of the kids at night, and Athena controls the rest by filling our social calendar to the brim."

"I feel you, my friend," Robert replied. "I have still to meet a married man whose social life isn't controlled by his wife."

The two men shared a nervous laugh that reflected the truth of that statement.

"Out of curiosity, what would you think about if you had time?"

"That's the problem, isn't it," Jack replied with animation. "Philosophy has become the shadow of itself over the years. Nine parts history and one part reflection on history. It has been ages since anything original came forth in the field. All the good thinking has already been done. Nowadays, philosophers are mostly institutionalized academics—like me—focused more on the politics of tenure than on philosophizing. It's a real shame. Philosophy was the original field from which all other fields emerged, everything from mathematics to biology to sociology to psychology—all of it was philosophy to begin with. That was why I fell in love with it in the first place. I wanted to belong to a group that pushed the envelope of traditional thinking, to work in a field in which new discoveries were made all the time. Instead, I am a teacher and a mediocre one at that."

"Come now," Robert responded. "You are a great teacher."

"No, I am not. My heart isn't in it. I just go through the motions."

Robert didn't want to repeat the flattery and sound patronizing, so he remained silent. Fortunately, Jack changed the subject.

"I've been trying to understand why you asked for that extra Council meeting the other night. What was that all about?"

A sad feeling came over Robert when he thought about Vigo. He'd told himself that he was trying to help the psychiatrist, but in reality, Robert needed to solve the puzzle to reclaim his own philosophical consistency. He didn't like to admit it, but Vigo had him confused and rattled. His meditation practice had already suffered. These days, he was avoiding the cushion when he could.

"You know, I am not supposed to tell you."

"Humor me, Robert. Please. I need something interesting to think about."

Maybe a philosopher can help more than any doctor can? Robert thought while looking at his best friend. I've already broken the doctor-patient confidentiality agreement with my wife. Why not him?

Robert looked around, leaned in, and whispered: "I can't give you too many details, but I was called in to consult with the mental hospital downtown."

"Dr. Burns?" Jack asked, enthusiastically.

Robert nodded.

"Welcome to the big leagues my friend," Jack said, patting Robert on the back, almost spilling Robert's Macchiato. The smell of coffee was heavy in the air.

"Well, it's not quite that simple," Robert added, unsure of whether or not to continue. "I'm not exactly in. I was just asked to consult on this one case…"

"…that involved meditation and death?" Jack interrupted with interest. He was leaning forward, his knees nearly touching his chin.

"Yes, that involved meditation and death. I've met the patient twice. He has been meditating for more than thirty years and is a board certified psychiatrist. He tried to kill himself," Robert said in a whisper.

"No way," Jack replied in a loud voice—too loud for Robert's comfort. "You're kidding right?"

"No," Robert whispered in response, moving his chair closer to Jack's. "Nobody understands why. I mean, I have meditated with the guy and it's the most peaceful experience I have ever had. It doesn't compute, does it?"

Jack leaned back in his chair and adjusted his round John Lennon glasses, carefully weighing the limited information Robert had given him.

"No, I agree, it sounds like nothing I've ever heard before," Jack finally replied, and again, his voice was too loud for Robert's comfort. There weren't all that many people in the coffee house, but breaking confidentiality made Robert feel uneasy.

"As I told you the other night," Jack continued, "there have been some accounts of people who have died willingly during meditation—although I can't say I trust any of those stories—but suicide? I've never heard suicide mentioned in the same breath as meditation."

Robert motioned Jack to come closer and keep his voice down.

"Oh, sorry," Jack said in a lower voice as he leaned in. "Did the psychiatrist explain why he wanted to die?"

"In essence, he said that he wanted to wake up from the dream of life, that he had uncovered the eternal soul and no longer needed his research tool, which is what he calls the human body," Robert answered, feeling relieved that he had finally decided to trust someone else with this information.

"Fascinating. He had been meditating for what, thirty years, you said," Jack marveled, shaking his head in disbelief, "and he tried to commit suicide?"

"That's what I kept repeating to myself for days after I first met him," Robert replied. "Even after I met him for the second time, I still can't say that I understand why. Why suicide? It seems to be the antithesis of everything that meditation stands for."

"Yes, the complete antithesis."

Empathy was a powerful thing. Jack's confusion was validating the emotional rollercoaster that Robert had been on since he first met Vigo.

"The truly perplexing thing is that I have never met anyone who can meditate the way he does. I mean, the peace, the depth, the serenity, it's astounding," Robert confessed. "In truth, I kind of like the guy even though I don't understand his motivation for wanting to kill himself. I even told Jessica the other night that he was the closest thing to a holy person I have ever met."

"The holy guy who wanted to kill himself? Do you know how insane that sounds?"

"That's exactly how Jessica responded."

"Who is this guy? What's his name?" Jack queried, his curiosity heightened.

Without thinking about the implications, Robert replied: "His name is Dr. Vigo Andersen."

"Vigo Andersen, Vigo Andersen," Jack echoed. "I know that name from somewhere."

"I doubt it," Robert replied, realizing that he had taken a step too far. "He didn't exactly socialize."

"But the name sounds so familiar. I wonder if he is connected to the university in some way."

"I couldn't tell you. I got very limited information about him from the hospital and we never talk much about his background."

"So, what are you going to do next?" Jack inquired, still trying to figure out where he knew the name from.

"I don't know," Robert replied with resignation in his voice. "I have googled this phenomenon extensively, tried every combination of suicide and meditation I could think of, and found nothing. I sat in the bookstore, close to my office, for almost an entire day earlier this week, leafing through books and magazines, trying to find clues, but so far, I have come up empty."

"Maybe you need to take a page from Arthur's playbook."

"What do you mean?"

"Maybe you need to talk to someone who has experience, you know, instead of only searching for answers in books?" Jack added like he was thinking out loud. "Remember how Arthur admonished me for being book-wise, but lacking experience?"

"Yeah, how could I forget?" Robert responded.

"Well, I think he had a point. Meditation is experiential. You should talk to someone who has dedicated their life to meditation, someone who lives and breathes it."

Robert felt stupid for not having considered this earlier.

Yes, he thought to himself, maybe the suicidal tendency of long time meditators is the dark secret that nobody talks about in public, but if I meet with someone who has experience, then...

"Of course!" Robert replied with enthusiasm. "That's brilliant. I don't know why I didn't think of this earlier. I'll contact the Buddhist Center in Westlake and see if I can find a Catholic priest who meditates here, like the one who taught me in Seattle. Thanks to you, I might actually be on to something here."

Chapter 18

"What does your schedule look like today?" Robert asked Jessica on their morning walk through McNaughton Park after dropping the kids off at school at 7.30 AM.

Fall had finally showed up. The temperatures were in the high sixties. There was a light breeze and the sunlight hit the trees at just the right angle for the leaves to glimmer. It was nothing short of perfect. Yet, both Jessica and Robert were preoccupied.

"I've got back to back meetings until noon, and then again until four. Can you pick up the kids after school?" she responded, walking briskly.

"Yeah, sure," Robert replied, breathing heavily. "What do you want for dinner?"

"Well, James did really well on his test yesterday and Cathy is flourishing in school. How about we let them choose?"

They both knew what that meant—a trip to the pizza buffet that the kids adored. It was an inexpensive way to reward them when they were doing well, although both Robert and Jessica were aware of how unhealthy it was.

What the heck, Robert thought, we can't be perfect.

"Sure," he replied.

"What about you? Got any interesting clients today?"

Robert had one client that morning, which was one more than the day before, but afterward, he was going to meet Father Thomas—a Catholic priest who he'd been referred to when he called the Seattle church he had attended all those years ago—and Daigen, an American Buddhist monk. He planned to be back early enough to pick up the kids.

The problem was that Jessica didn't know he was still working on the Dr. Vigo Andersen case. For some reason, Robert felt the need to keep that a secret.

"Nothing sensational," he replied. "Just the same, you know."

"Robert," Jessica said attentively, grabbing Robert's hand and slowing down, "is everything okay? You seem distracted. Is business picking up? You know that we talked about re-examining everything in the New Year. Are you getting a sense of how it's going?"

Yes. They had scheduled a meeting in January to decide if the therapy business was worth it or if it was time for Robert to get a regular job. He had been so preoccupied that he had forgotten about that.

"Everything is fine honey. I am distracted because I am thinking of all the new ways in which I am going to market the business. I think you'll be surprised when we look the numbers come January."

Why lie, Robert? Why lie? You know that lying is the alcoholics kryptonite, you can't afford it, the reasonable voice in his head screamed.

"Okay, but you promise to let me know if I can help you, right?" Jessica replied and gave him a tender kiss on the cheek.

She was being genuinely nice. She wanted to help. Robert felt like he had been punched in the gut. For an alcoholic like himself, lying was a dangerous proposition. It was the first time in his marriage that he had been deliberately untruthful. He didn't like it, but before he could come clean, he had to figure things out. He needed to find a way to make his therapy business work. He needed to solve the mystery of all mysteries, the case of the meditating psychiatrist who tried to kill himself. He would tell her the truth, but not quite yet.

Chapter 19

At the office that morning, Robert felt restless. How could he swing so dramatically from one emotion to the other? From deep peace to a dark void during his meditation sessions, from collected calm when he was with his clients to anxiety over his business, from intrigue to obsession over the Vigo case?

If he were a client, he would tell himself to calm down, to focus on one thing at a time, to get his act together, and most importantly, to come clean with his wife. Alas, he was not a prophet in his own mind. His train of thought was interrupted as his client arrived a few minutes before their session was supposed to begin.

Mark Evans was a thin man in his mid-thirties with a beard neatly trimmed in the same length as the hair on his balding head. His face was framed with black rimmed glasses and he wore the traditional Austin-wear, khaki shorts, t-shirt, and sandals.

Come to think of it, there really was no such thing as casual wear in Austin. Every day was casual. Robert was himself wearing his customary work clothes, a polo shirt, and long khakis, both black, going sockless in his Birkenstock sandals.

What would Mark's problem be? Robert wondered, trying to flex his emotional Sherlock muscles. Was it addiction, overwork, stress, anxiety? All of the above?

None of it interested Robert, not today.

"I am a stay-at-home-dad," Mark explained tentatively. "To tell you the truth, I really can't afford to be here," he added, "as we only have the one income, but I had to talk to somebody. I am increasingly lonely, bored, and irritated, you know."

Stay-at-home-dad? In my home, we call that the lead parent, Robert thought with cautious intrigue as he examined the client, who didn't look agitated, but rather resigned, beaten down.

"It was a dream come true for me when Anna and I decided to have kids. We have three lovely daughters, by the way," Mark continued. "After our first one was born, Anna suggested that I stay at home with the baby because she could get higher wages than I could, you know, with her degree and all. We didn't want to get a nanny from day one."

In my relationship, I have the degree, but my wife still earns more than I do, Robert thought, but of course, he didn't say that. He simply nodded and said: "Go on."

"I loved it at first, but recently I have begun feeling like an asexual being, a feminized male caretaker, an outlier in society, with no social group that I belong to, you know," Mark said, stroking his hair and beard nervously.

"For example, when I go to the store during the day, the women at the register ask me if I am not working today. If I say that I am staying at home with my kids, they say: Ahhh, isn't that nice, and that somehow lessens it," Mark continued, shifting in his chair.

"Then, when I go to the park with my girls, all I see are women with their kids, grouped together, yapping away while their kids play. I end up either playing with the girls or sitting on a bench watching them. Really, that's what my life has become, a watching and waiting game."

Yeah, we're all just watching the wheels go round, aren't we? Robert thought as the John Lennon melody started playing in his head. Why was it so hard for him to concentrate these days? Being present is the best present, he reminded himself.

"And don't get me started on creating playdates for the girls," Mark went on. "The other moms don't respond to me, so I have to ask my wife—who is working full time by the way—to contact them if I want a reply. Furthermore, when my wife comes home after a challenging day at work, I have nothing to say to her, except tell her about what the girls did, and when the day is done, let's just say that sex is always on the backburner. She is tired and quite frankly, I am not that interesting. I try to seduce her, but to no avail, especially since we still have a little one, a one-year-old, who can wake up at any moment."

Robert saw his own experiences reflected in what Mark was describing. The difference was that Robert had always been doing something on the side while taking care of his kids. Attending school. Trying to do a little bit of work. Nevertheless, he had gotten the same kinds of questions at the store, been in the same situations in the park, had trouble connecting with the mothers of his children's friends, and he understood the sex part better than he wanted to admit.

"Mark, I have been in a situation similar to yours, so truly, I empathize, but let me ask you this, how do you see life playing out if you don't make any changes to your situation?"

"I don't know," Mark replied, sounding exasperated. He ran both his hands from his forehead to the back of his neck. "I mean, I love my kids, don't get me wrong, but I am starting to understand why women fought so hard to get out of the house and into the workplace. It's a brain drain, you know, the simple, repetitive tasks, the sameness, the manual labor of cleaning and cooking, with no intellectual stimuli. I try to read and listen to interesting podcasts, but I don't meet any adults, except for my wife, and when she comes home, she is tired, and we have nothing to talk about."

Mark stared out the window. It was evident that he had a lump in his throat.

"If I want my marriage to work, I can't allow myself to grimace and gripe continually when Anna is finally home. I would love to run out of the house and do something for myself the minute she enters through that front door, but I also want to spend time with her, you know, even if it's not high quality."

"I understand," Robert said as he reached for the tissue box. He put it on the table between the two of them, just in case Mark would start crying. "You also said that you feel like you have been feminized. How so?"

His goal, as always, was to keep the client talking.

"Well," Mark answered hesitantly and took a deep breath to steady himself before he continued. "I guess I feel feminized because I don't see many men doing what I am doing. Strangely enough, in this day and age, cooking, cleaning and caretaking are still almost exclusively done by women, at least here in Texas. Maybe I would feel differently in another part of the country, another part of the world, but here I have no social group I can connect with, no other men doing what I am doing. It's beginning to get to me."

The loneliness felt by a social outlier, Robert thought. I can relate to that.

"I also find myself complaining like women in movies from the eighties and nineties, you know, saying things like, How come we never go out? Why are you so late for dinner? You come home and you are always tired, and so on. I mean, I am talking like a woman, my wife no longer sees me as a sex object, my kids often call me mommy... tell me that it doesn't sound like I am more a woman than a man."

"It doesn't, at least not to me, but I understand your frustration. I have been there as well. We, the male caretakers, are men doing things that women have traditionally done. It's a new frontier. We are explorers, boldly going where few men have gone before," Robert said, eliciting a sly smile from Mark for the *Star Trek* reference before he continued. "You see, Mark, women have been doing this for a long time. We have only just begun. We don't have the social skills or the support mechanisms in place. We need to create those on our own," he added, knowing all too well that it was easier said than done.

"Don't you think I have thought of that?" Mark replied, now leaning forward, his voice tinged with desperation. "Half my day is spent thinking about how I can improve my situation. I tried going to the gym, but the girls didn't like the daycare facility, which meant that getting them out the door became a hassle, so I quit. Then, I tried reaching out to the women in the park and going to mommy mornings at a local church, but I always ended up as the odd one out, either sitting alone or playing with their kids while the women gossiped."

There was anger in his voice as he kept talking.

"I have wanted to go out at night, but with whom? I tried talking to the other fathers in the area, but they all think I am taking a break from work, you know. They keep telling me that they envy me, saying thing like, Oh, I wish I could stay at home all day. They don't understand the tremendous work that goes into it. I have met two of them a few times over beer, but all they talk about is work and sports. When I try to talk about the kids, cooking, books, news, or something else, I hardly get a reply. I just feel so isolated. I never realized how much the social interactions at work and school meant to me."

Robert had gone through such periods of isolation. He had been saved by going to AA meetings and meeting the Council. Social isolation was a cause of many of the psychological issues that he encountered as a therapist.

Glancing at the clock on his wall, Robert realized that they were running out of time. He had heard the gist of Mark's dilemma—although there was probably much more to it—and he knew that Mark probably wouldn't be back because of his financial situation. It was time to deliver. He'd better say something good.

"Look, Mark," Robert said, "I understand your sacrifices, believe me, I do, but you have to remember that you made them for your kids. You decided to stay at home instead of sending them to daycare, didn't you?"

"I guess so," Mark answered.

"Has it ever occurred to you that you sacrificed too much?" Robert continued.

"Yes, that's one of the reasons why I am here. I feel like I sacrificed my social life, my masculinity, my sex life..."

"Yes, I get that, but now it's time for you to sacrifice more."

"What!?" Mark exclaimed, confused.

"You need to sacrifice more," Robert repeated. "You have to sacrifice the idea that you can always be there for your wife and kids. You need to sacrifice time with them to be able to have quality time with them—if that makes sense. You need to go the gym, the golf course, find a Meetup group that peaks your interest, or go out with the boys, even if you have to fake interest in sports or their work. You need to do something else than stay at home. Otherwise, you will end up ruining the very thing that you are sacrificing everything for."

"Okay?" Mark replied, sounding unsure.

"Make a list, a menu of sorts, of all the things that you could do on your own. Keep it handy. Whenever you get a chance, do something on that list."

Mark nodded like he was starting to buy into what Robert was saying.

"And you need to sacrifice something else," Robert continued, feeling like he was on a roll. "You need to sacrifice your ideas about masculinity and femininity. Instead of thinking about what you do as either male or female, just think about it as something that needs to be done and that you are the one doing it. Cooking, cleaning, and care-taking are not inherently male or female activities. Social norms have only labeled them such and you don't need to accept those labels."

The avalanche of words cascading out of Robert's mouth was meant for both of them. In fact, he was talking to himself more than anything else. Robert had gone through similar insecurities, especially after he had his vasectomy, feeling like less of a man. He had been playing around with the idea that male and female roles were primarily social labels for a while, and Mark had offered him the opportunity to articulate those ideas, even if they weren't fully formed.

Mark had left the office with a pep in his step, seemingly feeling better. Robert hoped it would last.

Chapter 20

On his way to meet the Catholic priest, Robert's mind was still focused on the session with Mark. He kept thinking about male and female roles, both the biological and social differences. Instead of preparing by making mental notes of relevant questions related to meditation and suicide, he kept asking himself: What does it mean to be a man in our society?

Himself a product of infidelity, Robert had been brought up with a weak sense of masculinity. Early in life, he had lived with his mother and spent a lot of time with his grandmother, both of whom were fine women that he considered his role models, especially when it came to caring for children, but they didn't exactly give him the masculine modeling he needed. During his formative years, he had only seen his father on occasion. Brock had been married to another woman.

Then, when Robert was eight, his world had been turned upside down when his father finally divorced his wife and came to live with Robert's mother. The four of them—his younger brother included, who was also a product of the now decade-long infidelity—had moved into a nice white picket fence house together and tried to pretend like they were one big happy family.

With his father in the home, Robert encountered an intensely masculine role model who was also an alcoholic. In retrospect, he saw that their relationship effectively messed up his ideas about a lot of things; including romantic relationships and the difference between what it meant to be a man and what it meant to be a woman. His father, the oversexed, adulterating, alpha male, was usually fun to be around — that is, when he was around. In fact, fun was all but guaranteed. Yet, at the same time, he was continually trying to get Robert to be more masculine, not at all happy with the sensibilities that his mother and grandmother had instilled. Be a man Robert, be a man, was the mantra that chimed at every possible occasion.

As a result, Robert became an overly masculine sexual being in his late teens and early twenties, a self-described conqueror of women, mirroring what he had seen his father do. The more Robert drank, the more he screwed around. The more he screwed around, the more harm he did.

He wasn't quite like his father because he often fell in love with the women he slept with and they fell in love with him. It was worse than screwing around without emotion because the girls would then hate him for breaking up with them when he fell in love with someone else.

He bounced around, like a sphere in a pinball machine, from one woman to another to another, usually securing a new relationship before he ended the previous one. He had a perfect excuse for his behavior — the environment he was brought up in. Of course I cheat, I was brought up by cheaters, unwittingly became his tagline.

Having created a trail of broken hearts and decimated friendships — after screwing around with one too many of his friend's girlfriends — Robert finally decided that he'd had enough. He quit drinking and did a complete one-eighty. He made an effort to be a good man, finally attracting a suitable mate in Jessica. He went on to become a husband and a father — roles he thought he would never play — but his ideas of masculinity got muddled along the way.

Being a man used to be a simple proposition. In hunter and gatherer societies, the difference was clear cut. The men hunted and the women tried to ensnare the best hunter for their survival and the survival of their offspring. Hunt and gather. Gather and hunt. Was that still what women were looking for? The best hunter?

Not his wife. She was the best hunter, metaphorically speaking. She hunted the equivalent of animals — she hunted money — and yet, she still wanted him to hunt her, at least, when it came to sex.

Was that the biological masculine and feminine? Did it all boil down to sex, just like his father had always said? No, he thought, it can't be that simple. Human beings are complex. Not everything boils down to sex, does it?

Disappointingly, that was how many women still saw men, as sexual predators when they were single or as sexual slaves when they were married, with the women providing or restricting sex, either tactically or whimsically, as they saw fit.

Robert's married male clients saw sex in an entirely different way than most women did. To them, sex was a way to genuinely connect with the women they loved, a way to satisfy their needs and to make them feel good. Sex was their primary way to create emotional connections. These men, himself included, were more concerned with their partner's arousal than their own. And studies confirmed that. Men were not the single-minded-sex-crazed-lifeforms they were often depicted as. No, they were more complicated than that. And yet, biologically, the difference between men and women was evident. Men manufactured testosterone and semen while women produced eggs and could carry children.

This is a procreation planet, Brock's voice echoed in Robert's mind. Be the best hunter and deposit your semen.

No wonder I sometimes feel emasculated, Robert thought. I no longer produce semen and I am clearly not the best hunter. Is my manliness lost? Men are no longer hunters and protectors. Women can do both of those things without us. They can even have children without us, via sperm banks, and they can surely have sex without committing.

The more he thought about it, the more unjust it seemed. Socially, women had grown into more roles, thanks to feminism — the idea of equality between the sexes, something he fully supported — but at the same time, men had lost roles. Some of them, like Robert and Mark Evans, who clearly put family first, had filled the vacancies left by the women by taking the caretaking and cleaning jobs that the women really didn't want.

If the family unit was to stay together, somebody had to do those jobs, right?

Men, in general, were lost in this brave new world of supposed equality, except maybe for alpha males and rich guys, who really were the patriarchy that militant feminists raged against. The softer men were lost.

Wasn't that most men nowadays though, he wondered as he drove into the church parking lot.

Chapter 21

Robert had been to a stone church, similar to the one he found himself in now, in Seattle, a few weeks after he had first gotten sober twenty years ago. As a newcomer in AA, he had been told to meditate and give his life over to God, so it made sense to go someplace that offered both worship of God and meditation. It had not taken more than a few sessions for Robert to realize that the Catholic Church had ideas about God that he wasn't ready to embrace. Yet, here he was again, looking for answers.

He was greeted by Father Thomas, a tall priest in his late seventies who wore the traditional black priest garb with a white collar. His silver-gray hair was neatly combed and yet it was evident by his bushy eyebrows, protruding nose hairs, and furry ears that he had not been introduced to any type of modern grooming equipment—or maybe he just didn't care.

"Yes, yes. I remember you. You called earlier this week and wanted to talk about Christian meditation, correct?" the aging Father Thomas said after Robert introduced himself.

"That is correct," Robert replied. "Thank you for seeing me."

"The pleasure is all mine, I assure you," Father Thomas replied. "Very few people seem to know about our contemplative practice in Christianity. I am glad to get a chance to talk about it. Let's go to the back room to get some privacy."

On their way, Father Thomas and Robert passed a church altar that was comprised of a marble slab and a twenty-foot cedar cross with a statue depicting the likeness of Jesus Christ being crucified. Above the cross were stained glass windows that let in a rainbow colored shimmer from the relentless Texas sun.

These guys really know how to make people feel small and inspire them at the same time, Robert thought. Maybe that is the key to religious inspiration? You are small and God is great. He is your father and will take care of you if you bow to him—through us of course. That was always the religious small print. God can only be reached through us. No matter how he spun it, organized religion wasn't for Robert. He had tried it every now and then, just to make sure, but it never stuck.

After descending a flight of stairs and walking through a narrow hallway, Father Thomas and Robert reached their destination—the staff breakroom. It was unassuming in direct proportion to the magnificence of the altar. The walls had been yellow at some point, but the paint was faded and chipped, showing the concrete underneath. The room—which could hardly have been bigger than fifteen square feet—was decorated with run down furniture, four plastic chairs, and a round patio table. A chest-high bench with a coffee maker and a worn microwave oven stood up against the wall. As they sat down, Father Thomas poured each of them a cup of coffee.

"What can I do for you my son?" Father Thomas asked.

I need to approach this with care, Robert thought. Not give too much away too soon.

"Well, as I told you on the phone, I am a therapist and I have a professional problem that I would like to consult with you about. Now, I know that you are not my priest, but can I assume that you will respect confidentiality?"

"Yes, yes, of course," Father Thomas responded like that went without saying.

"Great," Robert continued, glad to hear that confidentiality wasn't a problem. "Correct me if I am wrong, but when I called, you told me that there was a small group of you, Catholic monks and priests in Austin, that practice Christian meditation or contemplation, as you like to call it, every day, right?"

"Yes, there is a small group of us Catholics, maybe five or so, that have kept up the practice for more than thirty-five years now. There has only been one permanent addition to the group, as two of the older men passed away, but even as the core has stayed the same, we have occasionally invited guests to meditate with us."

"I have some questions related to that group practice if that is okay," Robert asked, taking a sip of his coffee. It tasted stale—like it had been made well before daybreak. The slight smell of mold in the room exaggerated the sensation. An old AC unit was working over-time to cool the room but wasn't doing a very good job. Both men were perspiring.

"Of course my son. I would be happy to assist you in any way I can."

"Alright then," Robert continued. "There is no easy way to ask this, so I am just going to come right out and say it."

Father Thomas nodded patiently.

"Of the men that have been meditating for twenty to thirty years or more, including yourself, have there been any instances of depression related to the practice, you know, periods of darkness and despair?"

"I assume you are referring to what we call the dark night of the soul, named so by Saint John of the Cross in the sixteenth century," Father Thomas answered near instantly, without blinking, without pausing, almost like he had expected Robert to ask this question.

The answer took Robert by complete surprise. He'd rather ex-pected to be on a fool's errand, but apparently Father Thomas not only knew about the depressive tendency associated with meditation, but he also had a name for it.

"I guess so," Robert responded, still mystified by the priests re-sponse. "How does this dark night of the soul express itself?"

"It varies slightly from person to person. I remember when I went through it," Father Thomas reminisced, "I had been meditating for almost twenty-five years and my meditation sessions kept becoming deeper, more peaceful. Then, as if from out of nowhere, my sense of peace was replaced with what felt like an abyss, a darkness that seemed like it was going to consume me. Over a period of several months, I became increasingly depressed."

The old priest paused for a moment, reliving those gloomy emo-tions. As he continued, the momentary depressive glare was replaced with a calming smile.

"It was thanks to the support from my group, and the larger community of Catholic priests and monks, that I got through that period. These days I look back on it with fondness. The darkness was eventually replaced with a profound sense of comfort, belonging, knowing. It was replaced with light."

"How did you get over this period of difficulty, this dark night? What did you do?"

"Well, first, my fellow priests reminded me of Christ's forty days in the desert. They told me that my soul was going through a similar period of purification. They underscored that the difficulty signaled spiritual growth. It was tremendously comforting," Father Thomas clarified. "When they were sure I understood what was happening to me, I was instructed to spend more time praying before meditation. I learned several special prayers—invocations of light and love—and my brothers also made sure that I never practiced meditation alone, told me that if we meditated together, they could make sure that I would not get lost in the abyss. They also helped me shorten the periods for which I meditated each day, from ninety minutes or so to no more than forty minutes. Finally, and most importantly, I was instructed to double my efforts when it came to caring for my fellow man. I spent more time caring for the sick and poor, consoling grieving families, and listening to the troubles of my congregants. I was told to serve in any way I could. I did that faithfully and think that made the deciding difference. The more I cared for others, the easier it was for me to turn my attention away from my internal demons."

Robert paused for a moment before he responded, gathering his thoughts.

"So, if I understand you correctly, Father Thomas, you are saying that, not only is this dark night of the soul a common occurrence, but also, that the brethren in the Catholic church—or at the very least the priests you associate with—have a method of dealing with it that consists of three steps. First, reframing the crisis as similar to Jesus's time in the desert, as a prelude to spiritual growth, second, increasing prayer and reducing meditation time, and third, serving your fellow man," Robert summarized. He had found that repeating what he had just been told significantly reduced the likelihood of misunderstanding.

"Well, I have never thought of it that succinctly, but, in essence, yes, that is what I am saying," Father Thomas replied, taking a sip of his now lukewarm and stale coffee. Robert could see him cringe a little as he swallowed.

"I guess that the number of people who practice meditation for long enough to experience the dark night is so small that the remedy has never been written down, rather passed down man to man," the priest added, reflecting on his own words, "but the three steps you just summarized might be worth writing down at some point. Who knows, maybe I will be the one to do that."

"I appreciate your willingness to share this information with me," Robert replied. "It has already been helpful. There is, however, one more question that I must ask—a question that is relevant to a case that I have been working on."

Robert paused in preparation.

"Father Thomas, to your knowledge, has anyone ever contemplated suicide or tried to take his life due to experiencing this dark night?"

"No, my son. Absolutely not. That has never happened to my knowledge," Father Thomas replied, sitting up. "You have to understand something about the Catholic faith my son. No matter how difficult things get, the sanctity of life is at the center of our beliefs. Only God gives life. Only God can decide when that life has run its course. The mere idea of suicide…"

"…are you saying that Catholics never commit suicide?" Robert interrupted.

"I am not that simplistic," the old priest replied. "What I am saying is that at the level of commitment needed to practice our type of contemplation, and to practice it for long enough to experience the dark night, you will only find the most devout among us. Within that group of practitioners, there is total respect for the sanctity of life, for God's creation. None of us would ever commit suicide."

"Not even in your darkest hour?"

"No, my son. Not even then. The sanctity of life is placed above all else."

Robert sighed. The conversation had provided some answers, but he felt like he had hit another dead end. Father Thomas sensed his deflation.

"Forgive me for prying my son, but is it by any chance you who has been contemplating suicide? Are your questions related to your own meditation practice?" Father Thomas asked Robert hesitantly.

As if startled from a daydream, Robert sprang to attention and immediately answered: "No. No. Absolutely not. My inquiry is purely professional. As I said, it has to do with a case I am working on."

"I must advise you to be careful when you meddle with these energies my son," Father Thomas said, looking at Robert like he saw something that Robert did not see himself. "When interacting with meditation, you are no longer working in the psychological world that you think you know so well. No. You have entered the spiritual plane. Without proper guidance, you are bound to get lost, just as I did. Remember to ask God to accompany you in your work."

"I assure you, Father, I am in complete control of the situation and I don't need any help from God," Robert replied as respectfully as he could muster.

He stood up and got ready to leave. He was lying through his teeth about the control, but he was not comfortable with the priest's suggestions and invocation of God. He didn't want to get into an argument.

"Thank you for everything," Robert said in an unsteady voice. "I need to leave now to get to my next appointment."

Why was it so easy for these men to get to him? Robert was used to being in control of his emotions and his reactions to other people, but these men, these long-term meditators… somehow… they...

"Of course my son," Father Thomas said. He got up, ready to escort Robert to the door.

"It's all right Father. I can find my own way out," Robert said, holding up his hand.

"Very well then," Father Thomas replied. "I will pray for you, my son."

Pray for me? I need concrete solutions, not prayers, Robert thought as he hurried to his car. He was disappointed. He had not gotten the answers he was looking for and he was no longer able to control his emotions the way he was used to. Hopefully, his next stop would provide better answers. At least, he could be sure that the Buddhist monk would not invoke God.

Chapter 22

Having traveled from one side of town to the other, Robert arrived at the Buddhist center, which was situated in a small suite within an upscale shopping area in Westlake, surrounded by high-end merchandise and health restaurants. Catholicism for the poor, Buddhism for the affluent and tech-savvy, Robert thought.

He considered himself lucky when he found a parking spot in the shade. As he stepped out of his Mercury, he was greeted by the toasty midday sun. The temperatures were in the low nineties. Trying not to sweat too much, Robert walked slowly towards his destination. Over the doorway hung a sign that read, *The Austin Buddhist Center: Tame Your Mind and Engage in All Possible Virtues.*

When Robert entered the cool and spacious open area, which was decorated in a colorful blend of orange, red and purple, he was hit with a strong smell of incense. Near the entrance was a small bookstore that sold Buddhist literature, incense, prayer beads, and statues, both wooden and bronzed. Robert recognized a couple of the bronze statues. He had bought similar ones when he first began meditating. Of course, they didn't help, not for meditation purposes anyway, but they made for lovely decorations.

The monk, Daigen—whose American name Robert later learned was Abner Friedman—was in his early fifties, short and chubby, with his head clean shaven, wearing the traditional orange robe of monks in his order. He greeted Robert by placing his hands in prayer pose and saying: "Namaskar, my fellow traveler. What can I do for you today?"

"My name is Robert Davis. I called earlier and made an appointment."

"Yes, of course, Mr. Davis. Come right in."

With the initial pleasantries behind them, Robert couldn't help thinking that there was something pretentious about all of this. Why would an American Jew take up an Eastern name, shave his head, and wear an orange robe? Fortunately, he was wrong, because as they spoke, he realized that Daigen was both knowledgeable and likable, that he wasn't pretentious at all.

The man had been a stockbroker in New York when he was known as Abner. He had bankrupted himself and several others during the dot-com era and had consequently fallen apart, both mentally and emotionally. With what little money he could scrounge together, he had retreated to Thailand where he'd spent the next eight years in a monastery and been reborn as the monk Daigen. His adopted name meant huge mystery and signified his willingness to grapple with grand philosophical concepts. Jack would probably like him. After the name change, the Lama at the temple had given Daigen the command to go back to his home country to help people relieve suffering through Buddhist meditation and righteous living. Daigen had been running this little Buddhist center in Austin for almost five years now.

The two men sat cross-legged on meditation cushions and sipped green tea while Robert quizzed Daigen about his meditation habits. The monk had approximately fourteen years of continuous practice under his belt and had studied with several meditation masters at the temple. His eyes shone brightly when he talked about his time in Thailand. He told stories about the temple, his fellow monks, the food, and the scenery. Robert almost felt sorry that the monk had been ordered to return to the USA. His heart clearly belonged to Thailand. When Robert finally asked about the meditation community that Daigen belonged to in Austin, there was a shameful pause.

"I am afraid I don't belong to any group of dedicated practitioners," Daigen finally answered. "I sit on my own daily and then I practice with my students, none of whom have been sitting for more than three years straight."

"That's too bad. I came here hoping to tap into the collective wisdom of your community," Robert replied, sounding dispirited. He suddenly felt like he was on a futile mission, a wild goose chase if there ever was one. Then he considered how Daigen's fourteen years of practice probably meant more in terms of experience than his own intermittent twenty years, especially since the monk had done nothing else while he was in Thailand.

"Maybe you can help me anyway," Robert added.

The monk bowed and answered: "I'll do what I can."

"I am looking into the phenomena of depression, apathy, even suicidal thoughts in relation to long-term meditators, people who have been practicing for twenty or thirty years, even longer. Did you ever hear about that at the temple?"

"Suicide? I can't say that I did, but apathy and depression among long-time meditators? Yes, I heard about that. The older monks sometimes talked about an obstacle during lectures, which they called getting lost in the emptiness," Daigen recalled. "Not relevant to beginners they said. I couldn't have disagreed with them more back then. Most of my eight years at the temple were spent battling emotions—sparring with the monkey mind, as they called it, letting go of internal distractions with almost every breath—and yet, when I compared my emotional rowdiness—which included periods of depression—with the idea of getting lost in the emptiness, they said it was not remotely the same thing. The kind of obstacle they were talking about came after the monkey mind had been tamed, when peace was the anchor, not while it was an unrealized dream."

"Did they tell you what to do once you arrived at this particular emptiness obstacle?" Robert asked, interested in learning more, wondering if their remedies were similar to what he had heard the priest explain earlier. Maybe the theology would be different, but the methods similar—at least, that was his hope. He couldn't hide his disappointment when Daigen answered.

"Yes, I did ask, but they refused to answer. They said: You don't need a boat until you come upon the lake. I remember it well because it's an idea I consistently use with my students. Most of them want to know everything up front. They are used to instant gratification. But I never tell them too much. Instead, I teach them a little bit at a time and then instruct them to practice. Only when they have practiced, do I teach them more. You see, a mind filled with premature or irrelevant information will not help a person find the peace that he or she is searching for," Daigen answered, obviously going into a rehearsed spiel that he had delivered many times before.

"So, you are okay with not knowing what remedies the older monks used to navigate through this obstacle?" Robert asked in dismay. "What will you do then, when and if you stumble upon this tendency to get lost in the emptiness?"

"I am not alone Mr. Davis, although I am on my own. I have a community back in Thailand that I communicate with all the time. I sit with them via Skype and learn from them at every opportunity." Daigen smiled knowingly. "Trust me, Mr. Davis. I will learn about the remedies when the time is right."

"I encountered a man the other day who had been meditating for more than thirty years. He tried to kill himself," Robert admitted, hoping that candor would spur some sort of response that could help him.

"Really? I am saddened to hear that. How did his community react?" the monk replied.

"He has no community," Robert answered.

"Isn't that the problem then?"

Robert felt like he had been slow putting two and two together. Community. That was one of the keys to Father Thomas's successful navigation through what the Catholics called the dark night. Daigen was trusting that his community would help him when the time was right. Vigo lacked community. Come to think of it, so did Robert.

"You think that having access to a community would have helped him?" Robert asked. "I never thought of it as that important. I mean, isn't community mainly inspirational and social in nature? I just can't see it as a central aspect of a meditative practice. I think you are suggesting that it is."

"Not central," Daigen replied, "but integral. Surely you must have learned about the four pillars of meditation at some point, yes?"

When their conversation began, Robert had told Daigen that he was a meditation practitioner himself, but he had left out the secular nature of his approach.

"No, I can't say I have. Early on, I learned basic meditation techniques, but I left out most of the philosophical and social elements. I didn't see their importance—saw them as superfluous."

"Well, then I feel obliged to share them with you," Daigen exclaimed immediately. "In the Buddhist tradition, we are taught that there are four pillars. One, meditation, two, introspection, three, community, and four, service. Permit me to clarify Mr. Davis," Daigen continued, without allowing time for Robert to respond. "The first pillar is meditation. It is defined as the practice of peace, of uncovering emptiness. It is the antithesis of unhappiness and suffering. Meditation creates happiness that is not dependent on outside circumstances. It creates internal bliss and is the central aspect of our practice."

Robert nodded and humored the monk by pretending to show interest in his explanation. His mind, however, was preoccupied. Why hadn't the Lamas trusted Daigen with the way to navigate through the internal obstacle of getting lost in the emptiness? It seemed irresponsible to send a dedicated practitioner halfway around the world without that information.

"The second pillar is introspection," the monk continued, "which is defined as the practice of self-appraisal, clearly seeing the obstacles that keep us from experiencing peace—everything from our own thoughts to our physical state to our surroundings. The third pillar is community, which is defined as the practice of mirroring, speaking truthfully about one's experiences, including obstacles, and comparing them to other people's experiences. When I speak truthfully, I often discover inconsistency between my thoughts, words, and deeds, and with the help of my peers, I can correct that."

Robert looked at the clock on the wall. Daigen's explanation was taking longer than he had expected. He needed to pick the kids up from school.

"The final pillar is service," the monk concluded, "which I have come to understand as the Buddha nature expressing itself in the world."

"What do you mean by Buddha nature?" Robert inquired.

"Itis difficult to explain," Daigen replied after a short pause. He looked like he was trying to be mindful of his words. "As I understand it, Buddha nature is the essence of what we experience in a deep state of meditation. It is oneness, calm, peace, emptiness. My goal as a monk is to bring that experience into the world. To serve others in that state of mind."

"To be peaceful in their presence and…?" Robert prompted.

"…and help them attain that same peace. Sometimes I do it through teaching, sometimes my being there is enough… and sometimes I fail because I do not feel the peace—the Buddha nature is hidden from me."

"And what do you do then?"

"I try not to make a mess," Daigen said, smiling mischievously, "and remind myself that I am a still a beginner, that every day I am a beginner."

"I don't want to get sidetracked, but this beginner's mind idea seems to somehow belittle experience—at least that's how I understand it," Robert replied.

"Beginner's mind is not about belittling experience. It is an attitude. When you are a beginner, you approach everything with wonder. You want to learn. I remind myself that I am a beginner because it is important not to lose the beginner's openness and zeal."

So, calling oneself a beginner was less about ability and more about attitude, Robert thought. Okay, he could live with that explanation.

"Are you absolutely sure you never heard the monks in Thailand talk about suicide or suicide attempts in relation to meditation?" Robert asked, grasping at straws.

"Not that I remember," Daigen replied.

"What about monks who willingly died during meditation?" Robert added.

"A couple of monks died during meditation when I was there, but they died because they were old, not because they sat down and decided to die. Where are you getting these ideas from anyway?"

The monk was visibly puzzled by Robert's line of questioning.

"Here and there. Some of them from my client, some from a friend, and some from the internet. I am sorry to keep bringing suicide into the conversation, but I am just trying to understand… " Robert responded. He realized that he wasn't getting anywhere. "I have taken enough of your time for now," he said as he stood up and got ready to leave.

"The only death I have heard about in relation to meditation is the idea of dying to the separate self," Daigen said as he stood up. It was clear that the monk wanted to help even if he didn't have the exact information that Robert was looking for.

"What do you mean by separate self?" Robert asked as they walked towards the door.

"Well, as human beings we compartmentalize," Daigen answered. "We think of the body and the mind as separate. We create all kinds of identities, as men and women, as fathers and mothers, as workers, as sports fans, as political participants, as lovers and spouses. Each role we embrace and identify with creates a new internal separation. We stop being able to express integrity because these roles are often in conflict with one another," he said rubbing his fists against each other to demonstrate. "For example, a father wants to give warmth, but an office worker needs to be resilient and guarded. The two are the same person. As a result of playing these opposing roles—and many others—that person experiences internal struggle. The struggle, in turn, creates unhappiness. It is through meditation that we die to these separate selves and create integrity. We settle down and realize that there is only one, that there is only peace. Letting go of false or limited identities can be hard—especially when we believe them to be the truth about us—but internally dying to the separate self has nothing to do with committing suicide, Mr. Davis. I really think you should reconsider your ideas and your sources. You seem a little confused."

How about a lot confused, Robert thought, as he thanked Daigen and exited the Buddhist center. His visits to the priest and monk had filled in some knowledge gaps, but the central question of how suicidal tendencies were related to meditation was still unanswered.

Chapter 23

That night, the Davis family was exhausted. As planned, they were at the kid's favorite pizza buffet place. The four of them sat there together but were not communicating. The kids were watching TV. Jessica was on her phone. Robert was lost in thought. They might as well have been miles apart. Typically, Jessica and Robert would, at least, be talking to each other while the kids were watching TV, but today the married couple hardly made eye contact. It was fine. Robert didn't know what to say. How would he explain his day to her anyway?

Darling, this morning I met a man who felt both marginalized and feminized, just like I have felt many times. The more I thought about modern masculinity, the less it made sense to me. The biology of being male and the social roles we play are no longer in sync. It kind of sucks.

Oh, and then I traveled across town, twice, to talk to a Catholic priest and a Jewish man, who is also a Buddhist monk, about meditation and how it might possibly be related to suicide. Both of them refuted the idea that suicide and meditation could be linked in any way, yet both also told me that it was normal for long-term meditators to go through periods of gloom and despair. Then the priest warned me about meddling in spiritual matters—told me to ask God for protection.

Yeah, that discussion would go well.

Robert looked around the dining room. Red and white tables were surrounded by yellow walls that were decorated with splashes of red, white and green, probably meant to denote the Italian roots of the pizza. He saw families of all shapes and sizes rolling in through the oversized doors. He noticed that without exception the men would pay for dinner and the women would help their kids get their meals — precisely the opposite of what Robert and Jessica had done.

I don't get it, Robert thought. Why is everyone still buying into these outdated social roles? Are we still stuck in the old model of man work, man pay, and woman take care of children?

He took a closer look at the men. Most of them were overweight and were wearing t-shirts marked with their favorite sports team. The Longhorns, Spurs, and Dallas Cowboys were the most common. Looking even closer, he noticed that none of them were smiling. Instead, they were either irritated or resigned—at least, that was Robert's take as he tried to flex his emotional IQ superpowers.

He felt sorry for them.

Sad, whipped, middle-aged men.

Sad and irritated. Muddling through life.

Poor guys.

However, as he observed them, it dawned on him. He was just like these slobs. He was overweight. He was not particularly happy. In fact, it was worse for him because he had tried so hard to be better than that. They were slobs because they didn't put in any effort. He was a slob despite all the effort he had put in.

Look at all the work I have done, Robert thought to himself, sensing the futility of his situation. The hours of therapy. The nightly meditation. All the books I have read. All the deep conversations about life I have engaged in. How I have embraced my caretaking role and become a feminist role model if there ever was one. And on top of that, I don't drink alcohol—a feat in itself. There is no excuse for my beer belly. I should be better than they are.

It was a known trap for alcoholics, thinking that because they didn't drink, because they were recovering, because they were working on themselves, then they should somehow be better than others. Robert hadn't fallen into that trap for a while, and now, the realization stung, just like a real trap would.

"Dad, can I get more," James asked, breaking Robert's reverie.

"Yeah, uh, sure," Robert answered. "Cathy, sweetie, you want something else?"

"No, thank you, daddy," she answered in her sweetest five-year-old voice.

What great kids, he thought. So polite. So content. At least, I seem to be doing something right there. At least, I am better than I would have been if I were drinking. At least, I am a better father than my dad was. Come to think of it, I should be content if I am better than I should be, considering my past. My life could have turned out so much worse. Maybe all the stuff I have done has kept me from sliding back into the familiar rut of drinking and cheating. Maybe it has kept me from getting worse.

Bing! Lights on. An epiphany if there ever was one.

My actions keep me from getting worse, but they won't continually make me better and better. That should be my new mantra. In fact, it should be a bumper sticker. It should be plastered all around my office… but then nobody would come, Robert quickly realized. People want to believe that they can get better and better and better and better. Heck, a part of me still believes that—wants that. Getting better all the time. Fake it 'till you make it.

He took another bite of his pizza.

"Daddy, I want dessert."

"Hmmm?"

"James, will you help your sister?" Jessica chimed in, still busy on her phone.

Robert's head was spinning.

There is melancholy, darkness, but they don't want to kill themselves. Beware of meddling in spiritual powers my son. Beware!? Woo, spooky. Was that supposed to scare me? The community saved me, the priest had said. Where is my community?

Weak men have been feminized. Be a man Robert! Shut up dad! Is that what I am, weak?

With all that I've done, I should be better, right? What's the point in trying? I'm just like these slobs around me. I might as well give up. No. No. My actions keep me from getting worse.

Spinning, spinning, spinning...

Chapter 24

Robert waited for Jessica to fall asleep before he attempted to meditate that night. His body was stiff, so he did a few stretches before he sat down. He arranged his blankets and cushion for maximum comfort, crossed his legs, straightened his spine and closed his eyes. He needed a break from his tumultuous thoughts; from the barrage of questions raised during his visits to the priest and monk.

Okay peace, he thought, as he assumed his best meditation posture, you may come.

It didn't. Not even close.

Instead, Robert's shoulders ached, his head felt heavy, his injured knee was throbbing more than usual, and his abdomen was roaring with discomfort from eating too much pizza. Yet, Robert sat, forcing himself into stillness.

I am not giving up due to discomfort.

The intense physical sensations functioned as an anchor for his mind. Robert tried to spin that into a positive, thinking that while the physical pain commandeered his attention, at least he wasn't caught up in the whirlwind of thoughts and emotions that had plagued him most of the day. But the longer he sat, the more discomfort he felt. His lower back began hurting, his shoulders were drooping, and, to his complete surprise, he felt a sharp stinging sensation around his heart.

No way, he thought. Am I having a heart attack?

The pain was sharp, penetrating.

Robert opened his eyes and felt around his heart.

Due to his family history, he'd had a conversation with his doctor about heart attacks a couple of years ago. The doctor had told Robert that if he could replicate the sensation by pushing on the muscles and ribs around his heart, then, in all likelihood, it wasn't a heart attack. Robert pushed. He prodded. The fact that his father had died of a heart attack at age sixty-six suddenly overwhelmed him.

I am relatively young for it to happen, but heart attacks at my age are not unheard of. Is this really happening?

Pushing. Prodding. Worrying.

"Ahhh," he couldn't help but sigh with relief when he realized that he could replicate the sensation by using his fingers.

I'm not having a heart attack. Good. I'm not ready. It's only pain, he told himself. Now, try to shake out the tension, breathe deeply, sit up straight and try to relax. Use your mantra, Robert.

One. One. One…

Arrrghhh, the body cried.

Robert couldn't focus his mind on the mantra for one moment. Nothing garnered his attention except the physical sensations, the discomfort, the pain. His knee stung, his back throbbed, his shoulders felt heavy like he was carrying the weight of the world on them, his head pounded, and his stomach felt like gremlins were boiling acid in there.

Okay then, he thought. If peace will not come, then my meditation practice tonight is to sit through discomfort. Instead of one, the physical sensations are my mantra.

And so he sat.

Attention moving from one painful sensation to another.

Chapter 25

Vigo was pacing slowly, walking step-by-tiny-step in a circle within the small space he had to work with, between his bed and the two chairs in his room. It was the first time that Robert had seen him out of bed—out of the lotus pose.

"Vigo. You are walking," Robert half-stated and half-asked in a surprised tone.

"Don't look so surprised Robert. The body still has needs. It needs to sleep. It needs to eat. It needs to go to the bathroom. It needs movement. It is one of the reasons why I am more than ready for my transition," Vigo replied, as he sat down in a chair next to his bed.

Robert sat down in the chair opposite him.

"I have news," Robert announced, "I have been to see a couple of people and I think I may have figured out what the two of us have been doing wrong."

"You mean, *you* think *you* have figured out what *you* think *I* have been doing wrong," Vigo replied, with unusual animosity.

"No. I meant what I said. I think I've figured out what *we* have been doing wrong," Robert reasserted.

"And what would that be?" Vigo asked arrogantly.

He seemed entirely different when he was not in his meditation posture.

"Well, for one thing, we don't belong to a community of meditation practitioners."

"And why is that a problem?"

"Well, the two long-term meditation practitioners I met told me similar stories about how they had been through periods of apathy and melancholy, just like the one that I believe you have been through—like the one that I seem to be going through. Their community helped them through those times, guided them through their difficulties. In addition, both men emphasized the role of service as a way to relieve their gloom and depression."

"And?" Vigo snarled.

"Well, I think that belonging to a group would help you and me mirror our ideas and stay grounded during times of apathy and despair. It would help us make sense of our experiences. And, most importantly, it would keep us from ever wanting to kill ourselves as there are no reports of suicide in these kinds of communities."

"You still don't get it," Vigo retorted forcefully. This was the first time during their interactions that the doctor was argumentative, angry. "You are still operating under the assumption that I was depressed and that was why I wanted to disrobe."

What a way to downplay suicide, Robert thought. Talking about it as disrobing, like the body was nothing more than a discardable piece of cloth.

"It is the opposite of that Robert, the opposite," Vigo continued with animation. "I found bliss, the eternal essence of my being. The body is the last obstacle that needs to be removed so that I can be who I really am."

"No Vigo! You are wrong!" Robert cried.

He had hoped his discovery about the importance of community and service would change Vigo's mind. Not in a million years did he expect this kind of animosity.

"You have embraced a philosophy that is convoluted and doesn't rhyme with anything I have found in other meditation traditions," Robert continued, both angry and frustrated. "Everyone else respects the sanctity of life. No one I have spoken to understands the link between meditation and attempted suicide. No one. Suicide and meditation don't go together. You are the one who is wrong! And I am telling you that you would have benefitted from belonging to a community. They would have exposed your delusions before they took hold. Like me, you have tried to meditate on your own and thought you were smart enough to figure everything out. You never compared your experiences with the experiences of other meditators and that is why you have come to this completely erroneous conclusion."

While Robert argued, Vigo climbed into bed and assumed his signature meditation pose. When Robert finished, Vigo was once again calm and composed.

"My dear Robert," Vigo said, now seemingly in a state of complete equilibrium. "We both know what you are doing. You are projecting. You fear that you have made a mistake by not belonging to a community. Consequently, you think I have made the same error. You fear death, and because I embrace my transition, even went so far as to instigate it, you want me to be wrong. You don't want to believe that the only reason for living is the unveiling of the true eternal self. You want life to have meaning on its own. Yet, the more you search, the more you realize that life doesn't have any inherent meaning. That scares you more than anything. The reason why you are frantically trying to solve my case is not for me—it is for you. You cannot bear to think that I might be right. But I am."

Vigo closed his eyes and entered his signature peaceful state. Robert could feel it and knew from experience that there was no way to get him out of it, but he didn't want to stop having this conversation. He wanted Vigo to understand that he was wrong.

"Vigo? Vigo?" Robert cried but got no reaction. "Come on. You can't just close the door on me you old fool. You are delusional and I have found out why. You disregarded community. You forgot that you are human, whatever else you think you are. You are the one who is scared. You are the one who is fleeing life. You are the one who needs help."

No response.

Chapter 26

Robert's laptop was open, a fresh new document was on the screen, and the cursor was blinking. Nothing came to his mind. Nothing!

It was the beginning of October already. That morning he had looked at his schedule for the coming month. The first week, four clients. The second week, two clients. The third week, one client. One. For an entire week. To make matters worse, it was the only new client he had this month. His base wasn't replenishing fast enough and his current clients were becoming too self-reliant.

Roll up your sleeves boy. Do some regular hard work for a change, his father's voice said in his mind. Screw you, dad! Look where hard work got you. Dead at sixty-six.

The knot in Robert's stomach tightened. He was probably too late to save his business—at least if the deadline was January. He knew from experience that any marketing he did, especially networking, took too long to convert into paying clients. He really shouldn't have closed shop to operate a summer camp for his kids. That was when the drop off had started. He rolled his eyes in defeat. The marketing he didn't do that summer would have been bearing fruit now.

Sowing and reaping.

Reaping and sowing.

Laws of nature were a bitch.

Since he was being honest with himself—for a change—he knew that the summer break hadn't been his only problem. His obsession with Vigo had completely thrown him off balance and was still affecting him.

Vigo!

Robert hadn't seen him for a week. After he had tried to suggest that lack of community was Vigo's central problem, he'd gone to see him one more time, and that time, the good doctor hadn't moved a muscle, just stayed in a deep state of meditation. Robert had tried to meditate with him as he had done in the beginning, but it was as if a barrier had been created between the two of them. Robert didn't sense the same kind of peace emanating from Vigo as before. He felt locked out.

Nonetheless, he had decided to give Vigo's case one more shot. Earlier in the week, he had made an appointment with his friend, Jack, this coming Sunday, to go over the case once more, to see if Jack would notice something that he hadn't seen. Jack had called yesterday to tell Robert that he had found something that would blow Robert's mind, so Robert was cautiously excited, but he had simultaneously made the decision that if nothing new was uncovered, if he didn't make a breakthrough in the case, then he was surrendering, giving up. In the end, he might have to come to terms with the fact that this case was unsolvable.

Rats! He had blocked an entire Friday in his calendar, put it aside to develop a marketing strategy, and yet, here he was, still thinking about that doggone meditating psychiatrist. Strategy, Robert. Strategy! Focus. You will lose the practice if you don't come up with a plan.

But what to do? He examined his options as he stood up and paced the floor.

Should he place ads in the paper? No, the stupid local papers wanted him to sign up for the minimal amount of five hundred dollars a month, every month, for a year. He couldn't afford that. Even Facebook and Google ads were out of his reach. Marketing with no money? What was he thinking? It was impossible.

What about social media? Could that give him the extra push he was looking for? He had tried blogs, tweets, and posts, but even when his posts got reaction it never translated into paying clients. He had spent an inordinate amount of time in virtual space, where everyone was shouting, trying to get noticed, but it hadn't worked, except to irritate him. Nevertheless, the idea was persistent, probably because it was free.

What if I try social media one more time, he thought. Maybe I've been doing it wrong. I mean, I haven't exactly put one hundred percent effort into it. I could use the roll out plan and advanced techniques I learned in a social media masterclass webinar this spring.

No, the reasonable voice in his head screamed in protest. Not one more minute on social media. That won't save the therapy business.

Standing behind his desk, Robert stared at the blinking cursor on the empty computer screen. He had not written down one workable idea. Not one. His frustration grew as he walked to the window and stared at the leaf covered parking lot outside. He bit his lip and tensed up. Think, damn it, think!

He'd been avoiding the final idea. It had been in the back of his mind for a while, but he had not wanted to entertain it. Ugh! The thought of having to call people in desperation, of receiving rejection after rejection, was more than he could bear. How did Jessica do it—talking to people all day, he wondered. Maybe high-end sales were different? Maybe, if he had someone like her on his team, maybe then it would work? But him? Calling, asking, offering, begging? Not in your life.

Why don't you throw in the towel, you loser? Again, his dad's voice interrupted his train of thought. You have one chance to save your business and you won't take it? What's wrong with you?

Yeah. What was wrong with him? Why didn't he just bite the bullet, pick up the phone and start calling?

He walked away from the window and sank into his chair. He had tried to be a salesman earlier in life, had even gone through a couple of trainings and read a few books. Fear is false evidence appearing real, one of his trainers had said. It made sense at the time, yet, as soon as he had begun working—whether it was cold calling or chatting people up in stores—that so-called unreal fear had gotten a hold of him and the anticipation of being told no caused excessive emotional turmoil. Consequently, he'd quit those jobs and instead looked for a line of work that didn't constantly involve being told no. Except, now it did—that is, if he wanted to keep his business.

Was that really what he wanted? To stay in this business? To be a therapist in private practice?

Yes. Being a therapist was awesome when it worked. He liked the lifestyle, the odd hours, the variety of cases, not having a boss, and spending some of his hours at the bookstore or coffee house. At the same time, Robert had to admit that he had never been cut out for the other half of owning a business, especially the marketing and accounting parts. By owning his own business Robert had hoped to escape the punch clock, the overbearing step-by-step processes, the endless paperwork, the inept bosses—you know, all the things that people don't like about having a job. What he hadn't fully realized when he started the business, was that by jumping into the deep end, he had sacrificed security and stability. Most importantly, he had not realized that the market forces were a much harsher boss than he would ever have to serve under in the real world. In this business, survival of the fittest wasn't a metaphor.

Despite all of that, my answer is still yes, he thought. Yes, I want to own this business. I want to make it work. I want to prove, to myself, to my wife, and to my dad, that I have what it takes. All I need is a little more time. I will come up with a strategy that works, one that doesn't involve the humiliation of calling people. I can do this.

But, when it came time to leave for home that day, the knot in his stomach was still there and the cursor on his blank computer screen was still blinking.

Chapter 27

Lying to Jessica felt horrible. Robert wanted to tell her that his strategy session had been an absolute failure, that he only had seven clients booked for the entire month of October, and that he was still working on the Dr. Vigo Andersen case, but for some reason, the time had never presented itself. When she asked how everything was going at the dinner table on Saturday, all he could do was answer, fine.

The four of them sat at the dinner table, eating grilled chicken thighs, corn on the cob and coleslaw, drinking sparkling apple cider in tall glasses, having a conversation with each other. No TV. No cell phones. Just the four of them. These were the moments that Robert lived for under normal circumstances, but his inner battle was obstructing what should be feelings of joy and gratitude.

For all intended purposes, it had been an exemplary family day. They had woken up around 8.30 AM. He had made pancakes and bacon. At noon they had ventured out into the comfortable fall weather, temperatures in the mid-seventies, taken a stroll around a nearby lake, and the kids had played for almost an hour at the playground while Jessica and Robert threw a Frisbee. After the outing, they had bought ice cream and driven around with pop music blaring on the stereo for half an hour. Then Robert had manned the grill for a little over seventy minutes, while the kids played in the yard, using the orange cones he had bought for them to create obstacle courses and timing themselves as they ran through them. And now they were eating dinner. It was the perfect day, right?

Not for Robert. He didn't feel well at all. Instead of participating fully, he had gone through the motions. He had been irritated when it took longer than usual to get the family out into the car as they were leaving for the lake—not that they were in a hurry. He had barked at Jessica when they were playing with the Frisbee disk, accusing her of not putting any effort into it. He had been obsessed with the kids not spilling ice cream in his car instead of letting them enjoy the experience. And while grilling, he had given everyone the silent treatment, fuming in his own internal anguish.

Disappointment was a word too soft to explain how he felt. With every mistake he had made over the course of the day, he had chipped away at the joy displayed by his family and had consequently become more sullen. He was not fine in any sense of the word. Yet, that was how he replied when Jessica asked him. Fine.

Of course, she didn't buy it. Neither did the kids, who couldn't wait for dinner to be over so that they could do something on their own. They had picked up on his short fuse early that day and tried to make the best of it.

He needed to snap out of it. If not for himself, then for his kids.

"Let's make a toast," he said, raising his tall glass of cider. "To grumpy dad, who promises not to be grumpy for the rest of the evening. How does that sound?"

The kids responded enthusiastically with a yay while Jessica just smiled as her glass touched his during the toast. He felt lucky to have her.

He had worked on that technique over the years, calling himself out, making the apology a part of a joke. Sometimes it worked, sometimes it didn't. Tonight it did. Instead of each of them spending the night in their own corner, the Davis family sat on the sofa, snuggled together, and watched *101 Dalmatians*.

That moment reframed the entire day for Robert. If not for the grumpy admission and the close-knit family time that followed, he would've considered the whole day ruined. Now, he would look back on the day with semi-fondness. What a difference a moment makes.

After the kids went to bed, he even snuggled up to Jessica and stroked her hair. They watched a romantic comedy of her choosing. One thing led to another and they ended up making love for the first time in two weeks while looking deeply into each other's eyes.

What a turnaround. He still didn't feel well—feelings of confusion and guilt still gnawed at him—but this evening had been a welcome reprieve from his emotional distress.

Chapter 28

Bweee. Bweee. Bweee.

It took Robert a moment to realize where he was.

Bweee. Bweee. Bweee.

He was at home. His alarm was going off.

Bweee. Bweee. Bweee.

He looked at the clock. It was 8.45 AM on a Sunday. He turned off the alarm and crawled out of bed. Jessica didn't stir. She planned to sleep in today. So did the kids. Robert was scheduled to meet with Jack at 9.30 AM. His head felt foggy. He brushed his teeth and got dressed in his black jogging pants and Batman t-shirt—his favorite weekend wear. Then he grabbed a raisin and cinnamon English muffin for breakfast and brewed a Keurig cup of coffee into his stainless steel travel mug. It was a little after 9 AM when he rolled out of the parking lot in his Mercury.

He wasn't exactly sure how he could benefit from meeting with Jack to discuss the Vigo case, but Jack was adamant. He'd called near the end of the week to tell Robert about his discovery—refused to disclose what it was—and again on Saturday to confirm. That was very unlike the otherwise stoic Jack.

At 9.25 AM Robert was standing outside of Jack's door. He lived in a brick house in North Austin. Jack came running to the door in his underwear.

"Robert! You're early! I knew you would be," Jack said excitedly. "I should have gotten dressed. Get comfortable in the dining room. I'll put some clothes on in a jiffy."

Jack ran into his bedroom. His mannerisms were decidedly un-Jacklike.

"Sure," Robert replied.

Once dressed, Jack joined Robert at the shiny, oval dining room table.

"Here we are Robert," Jack said ceremoniously. "The stage is set. No wife. No kids. Just two willing minds, ready to engage in a deep, meaningful, philosophical discussion. I wish that every day could be like this."

"What has gotten into you, my friend?" Robert asked out of curiosity.

"You'll see soon enough," Jack said, trying to look calm. "Now, as you know, I have something to share with you, but why don't you begin by summarizing your thoughts about the case? I know the ins and outs, but it would be great if you could refresh my memory."

"Why don't you tell me about your discovery first," Robert responded, yawning.

"Please, humor me."

"Okay. Here are the facts," Robert said, feeling both, impotent, because of his lack of progress, and heavy hearted, because of the inner chaos that the interactions with Vigo had caused him. Reluctantly, he outlined what had transpired.

"Dr. Vigo Andersen is a trained psychiatrist who has been meditating for over thirty years. He tried to kill himself. Now, I always imagined that any person who was ready to commit suicide would be in some sort of pain, physical or emotional, but that doesn't seem to be the case with Vigo. In most of our interactions, I have been the emotional one while he maintains peace and equilibrium. There is no apparent pain and he doesn't seem to be running away from anything. Rather, he appears to be driven by the philosophy that the goal of life is to uncover an everlasting self—something he claims to have done—and that is why he says he is now ready to discard the body, which is really just a tool in his mind. He talked about dying as disrobing the other day. Disrobing—like the body is just a piece of clothing, not a vehicle of life."

Jack listened intently.

"I have tried to challenge his assumptions," Robert continued, "but, unfortunately, I haven't found any meditation philosophy that rhymes with his ideas. Both the Catholic priest and the Buddhist monk I met with refuted the idea that meditation practitioners could ever be suicidal, and, as I told you the other day, the internet is oddly silent when it comes to this. To be honest Jack, I am at the end of my rope. I would love to solve this case, but..."

Robert fell silent, feeling completely deflated.

Jack reached over to the chair beside him, picked up a book, turned to a bookmarked page and handed it to Robert.

"Here. Read this."

"What is it?"

"It's a second-hand copy of the *Bhagavad-Gita*," Jack replied. He couldn't hide the excitement in his voice. "Read it. Out loud."

Puzzled, Robert began reading.

"Know this Atman. Unborn, undying. Never ceasing. Never beginning. Deathless, birthless. Unchanging forever. How can It die the death of the body?"

Robert looked up from the book.

"This sounds eerily like Vigo."

"Continue reading," Jack urged.

"Worn-out garments are shed by the body. Worn-out bodies are shed by the dweller." Robert looked up again. "So that's where he got his idea of disrobing from."

"That's not all," Jack added excitedly. "Turn to the front. Look at the insignia."

Robert turned to the front page.

"No!" he exclaimed. "It can't be. This book is marked as belonging to Vigo Andersen. Are you kidding me?"

"It's true," Jack said, grinning ear to ear. "Remember when we met at the coffee house and I said that I knew his name from somewhere? This must be it. I picked this book up a couple of years ago at a used bookstore in town, but it was only this week that I made the connection."

Robert was stunned.

"I knew that you had looked into Buddhism and Christianity for explanations," Jack continued, "but I figured that you might have forgotten about Hinduism, so this week I started leafing through this copy of the *Bhagavad-Gita* for similar ideas. That's when I found the passage you just read. Imagine my surprise when I saw the inscription… well, I guess you don't have to imagine, do you? You seem to be having the exact same reaction as I did."

"What are the odds?" Robert said incredulously, still examining Vigo's handwriting.

"That was my reaction at first," Jack responded, "but as I thought about it, it wasn't as far-fetched as I originally imagined. I mean, how many people in Austin are interested in this sort of philosophy? Not so many. For me to have picked up a copy that previously belonged to him, well, let's just say the odds aren't as astronomical as our initial reactions would suggest."

"But for you to find it at this moment," Robert replied. "What does this mean?"

"I asked myself that as well," Jack replied. "It is natural for us to look for meaning in everything. Looking for meaning is distinctly human. For a while there, I let my mind go wild and conceived some rather fantastical explanations, but now, in my down to earth interpretation of the situation, it simply means that we now know where he got his ideas from. People, like our friend Arthur, would probably read more into it than that, but we are men of science Robert. This was just a lucky coincidence — yes, mind blowing and cool — but a lucky coincidence nonetheless."

"You can say that again," Robert said, sighing in astonishment, "but, if this is where he got his ideas from, then that only strengthens my theory that meditation fortifies whatever philosophy the practitioner has when he starts meditating. I was hoping I'd been wrong about that — you know, just because of the implications."

"What do you mean?" Jack asked, leaning forward.

"It's an idea I have been entertaining for the past few weeks," Robert explained, sounding somber, the elating effects of finding Vigo's inscription wearing off quickly. "I haven't figured out all the details, but it seems to me that a person's belief system is strengthened through the practice of meditation. You know, for example, that I have a secular view of the world, and so, to me, meditation has always been about creating moments of peace — at least, that's what I believed until

117

I met Vigo. He, on the other hand, believes in this Atman idea, about an everlasting soul, which is somehow more real than the body and mind, so voila, meditation confirms that for him. And yet we are both having the same meditative experiences, or so I think."

"You are saying that meditation is highly interpretive and that the interpretation depends on the ideas that a person has prior to starting to meditate," Jack said as if to explain the idea to himself. "I've thought along those lines. It sounds plausible."

"I guess," Robert continued, "I mean, the meditation technique seems to be one thing, the physical, emotional and mental experiences it produces another, but then each person's interpretation appears to be the third and most important component. If true, then the profound peace produced during meditation is like a blank canvas, it doesn't really mean anything."

Even though Robert felt like he was thinking and communicating clearly, he was slowly being overtaken by dark and dreary emotions, drawing him deeper into an emotional swamp with every minute that passed. Why was he feeling so wretched?

"The idea would explain a lot of things," Jack replied. He was not giving Robert's emotional state much attention. "For example, the difference between what you and Arthur were saying the other night; his dualistic, light versus dark interpretation, opposed to your non-dual one. It would also explain why people who meditate together in groups seem to interpret their experiences similarly. They already believe in the same philosophy, myth or theology."

"I guess… " Robert replied. For some reason, he was bothered by the fact that Jack was supporting his theory.

"Well, my friend, it sounds like you have cracked the case."

"How so?" Robert answered in a sour tone.

"Well, as I see it, Dr. Andersen took the idea of the Atman, the un-changing soul, which is said to discard bodies and dress in new ones, to its illogical conclusion, that life doesn't matter, which, by the way, is definitely not the central message of Hinduism. He disidentified with the body-mind and identified strongly with the meditative state instead. To him, the meditative state was the eternal soul. The more he identified with the Atman, the less he identified with the body until he finally decided that the body was longer useful and tried to kill it. Case closed, right?"

"It sounds so straightforward when you put it that way," Robert replied defensively, "but you haven't met Vigo, Jack. He is utterly convinced that he is right. He seems to think that it is all of us who are delusional, and, even after everything that has happened, I have to admit that he is convincing, not just because of how he talks, but also because he achieves a deeper state of meditation than anyone I have ever met. That is how he got to me. He's still getting to me I guess, because even though my theory sounds intellectually sound, I am not completely convinced."

"Being persuasive doesn't mean anything," Jack exclaimed, clearly frustrated by the fact that Robert wasn't embracing his own theory. "There are plenty of delusional people out there who are convincing—conspiracy theorists, politicians, priests, self-help gurus—the list is a mile long. Just because a person has a deep conviction, doesn't mean they are right."

"But it's more than that Jack. It wasn't just Vigo that went into a deep state of meditation. It was also me. If it all comes down to subjective interpretation, then how come I never experienced such a profound state of meditation before I met Vigo?"

"I don't know why he influenced you in such a way," Jack replied, his frustration growing, "but you can't read too much into it. The fact that you achieved a deeper state has nothing to do with the incomplete and wholly erroneous ideology that Dr. Andersen has embraced. Even though he may have access to deep states of altered consciousness, it doesn't make his decision to commit suicide any less deluded."

"But…"

"Let me finish. Maybe he has mastered a meditation technique, but his philosophy, his interpretation—as you suggested—is completely off the wall. Try disengaging the two in your mind and you will see that you have solved the case. Meditation technique or not, he attempted to kill himself. You wouldn't claim that a virtuoso musician that tried to kill himself could set any type of precedent. His ability to play music and his attempted suicide would be treated as totally separate things, right? Then why treat Vigo's ability to meditate as somehow connected to the fact that he tried to kill himself?"

"Because he says that the two are connected," Robert cried, "and for some reason, a part of me believes him, even if I have come up with what seems to be an entirely rational explanation."

"Look, Robert, you deal with human beings all day. You know from experience how people can convince themselves of the most ridiculous things. Maybe Dr. Andersen needed to believe that the body was discardable to escape the pain of living? Maybe he buried whatever pain he was hiding, his real reason for wanting to die, so deeply in his subconscious mind that the pain was no longer visible to himself or others? Maybe that's why you detected no pain? I don't know. I am not a psychologist. What I do know is that his philosophy is incomplete. He borrowed a little bit from Hinduism, but he did not take the entire philosophy into account. The Hindus have wonderful ideas about love, service, and intellectual stimulation to go with their core concept of an eternal soul. To them, life has a purpose. Whatever you do, you can't overlook the fact that Dr. Andersen's philosophy is one of apathy and utter detachment, that it resulted in his attempted suicide. Even if your personal meditative experiences may have been triggered by him, you shouldn't let him influence you in such a way. Robert, my dear friend, this case is closed. You have solved it. Be happy about that."

Robert looked at Jack and shook his head. He felt empty, not the peaceful kind. No, it was like a void. What Robert imagined a pressure chamber in space would feel like if all the oxygen were sucked out. Right now, he was in that chamber without a spacesuit—suffocating.

If Robert was right, then meditation didn't mean anything. If Vigo was right, then life was a dream. Either way, the cornerstone of his emotional wellbeing for the last twenty years was being dismantled in front of his eyes. His belief that meditation provided moments of peace had been swept off the mat.

Robert stared at the shiny oval dining room table. On the glossy surface, he noticed his own reflection. Eyes empty. Face pale. He looked like he had just been told that a close relative had passed away.

Chapter 29

It had been three weeks since Robert had seen Jack. He didn't feel any better. In fact, he felt a lot worse about everything. Today he was seeing the one client he had all week. One! She was also his only new client in a long while. Next week, he had no bookings. Nonetheless, he went to the office every day, hoping that Jessica wouldn't suspect anything.

To make things worse, Robert had stopped meditating altogether. He couldn't shake the feeling that if he kept meditating without belonging to a community, without embracing a complete philosophy that gave meaning to the empty meditative state, then he would end up the same as Vigo had, either dead or in a mental hospital. It was ironic because that was exactly what was said about the fate of alcoholics who didn't find sobriety—that they would either die or go insane. But, instead of trying to find a complete philosophy, or at the very least embrace the community that he had access to already, Robert had done the opposite and isolated himself. He hadn't been to an AA meeting for two months, hadn't kept his bi-weekly engagements with Jack, and the Council hadn't met since September.

Now, he sat in his unpaid leather chair—a constant reminder of his failure—and stewed in rotten emotions. It was like he had fallen face first into a filthy puddle, but rather than rolling over and getting up, he continually pushed his face deeper into the muddy water. It was a poor me festival if he had ever thrown one. He was viewing life through a pair of self-pity glasses. All the sacrifices he had gladly made for his family just weeks prior, he now saw as heavy burdens that he could hardly muster the energy to perform. His degree, which he had been so proud of when he graduated, he now believed to be worth less than the paper it was printed on. Instead of seeing that the love of his life was sticking with him through thick and thin, he imagined himself trapped in a passionless relationship with Jessica.

The Council was a joke and his AA meetings were full of re-hymenated holier-than-thou addicts that were quite frankly beneath him and his twenty years of sobriety. Everything that once tasted sweet was now sour.

It was into this atmosphere that she walked, Debra Flanagan, a stunning redhead in her late thirties, flaunting her full, glistening lips, long legs, curvy hips and perfectly shaped breasts. She wore a snugly fitting red designer dress and shiny black high heels. As she swung her Gucci handbag over the back of the chair, sat down, and crossed her legs in the most feminine way imaginable, Robert became exceedingly self-conscious. He hadn't freshened up at all that morning. His breath probably stank. His clothes were from the day before— hopefully, there weren't any stains, he didn't dare to look—and he was going barefoot in the office, his Birkenstocks tucked away under his desk. In the presence of such a gorgeous woman, his masculinity took a harsh blow, like he had been punched in the gut. She was so far out of his league that he didn't even feel like he belonged in the same room as her. His emotions sank to a new low.

Act professionally Robert, the reasonable voice in his head said loudly enough so that he snapped out of it—at least long enough so that he didn't make a complete fool of himself.

During the first few minutes of the session, the two of them went through the normal pleasantries. Robert found out that Debra was an attorney, married, with two children, but because of her work she had to travel quite a bit—just like his wife, Jessica, had to do for her work.

"So, what can I do for you, Mrs. Flanagan?" Robert asked, trying to deepen his voice and sound like a professional, simultaneously attempting to hide that fact that he was barefoot by tucking his feet under the chair, but she had probably noticed by now. Women always noticed such things.

"I think that things are about to become very difficult at home," Debra explained, crossing her arms, accentuating her already exposed cleavage. Robert felt uneasy. He could usually quell feelings of arousal in the presence of female clients, but he had let down his guard in the emotional state he was in. She was hot.

"How so?" Robert asked, focusing on Debra's flaming red hair to draw attention from her sensual outlines.

"Well, I never meant for it to go this far. I mean, it started quite innocently," she proceeded to explain. "Over a year ago, I signed up for Tinder, not to have an affair or anything, but just to see who would be interested in me. It was flattering, to say the least."

Why would a woman like you need that? Robert thought. You probably have to fight off more sexual advances than you care for. If I weren't married, if I weren't your therapist, I would... but, of course, he didn't say any of that, rather he went through his usual motions, nodded and said: "Go on."

"I must admit," Debra said, smiling shyly, "I feel a little uneasy telling you this, but I have to tell someone. I think that my marriage is on the line."

"You are completely safe here," Robert replied, trying to reassure himself at the same time. Underneath he felt a torrent of emotions. His self-deprecation sunk to a new low. He knew that if he were to act on his sexual arousal with this woman, she would surely reject him. At the same time, he felt ashamed for feeling anything towards her; ashamed for having let down his guard enough to allow inappropriate erotic sensations to arise. Cheating was way outside of his moral zone. Images from his adultery ridden childhood flooded his mind. He knew how much damage cheating could do.

Shame on you, Robert. Shame on you.

"Thank you for reassuring me," Debra replied. "As I was saying, it was all good fun to begin with, but as my traveling increased, I signed up for a website for people who wanted to have affairs, again just to see who would be interested."

I don't like where this is going, Robert thought, realizing that he had been distracted by his own arousal and feelings of inadequacy, not really listening to her until now.

"The number of men who were interested in my profile was over-whelming and well, exciting. So, I decided to meet a couple of them. One thing led to another, and... before I knew it, I was hooked. The excitement. The romance. The sex. It was all so adventurous. I felt more alive than I have in years."

You cheating bitch! Robert responded mentally, biting his lip.

He was reminded of his mother crying herself to sleep, of endless fights, of his father calling and asking angrily where his mother was when she wasn't home. The images kept coming in an internal cacophony of sounds and emotions—an eruption of memories from the recesses of an undeveloped mind deeply scarred by betrayal. Debra must have realized that she had disturbed him somehow, even though he thought he was doing a good job of hiding his extreme feelings of disgust and anger.

"It's not that I don't love my husband and children Mr. Davis. No, I love the three of them very much. I just see a difference between loving and wanting. Having these affairs was just something I wanted, something I needed to do for myself—it had no impact on my love for them," Debra explained, apparently feeling ashamed for displaying unbridled passion when she spoke of her affairs.

It took all the energy Robert could muster not to scream at her, not to drive her out of his office. His childhood emotions of insecurity and distrust rushed to the front of his mind, clouding his judgment, uniting with an already gloomy emotional state. She clearly had no idea how much pain she could cause other people by her behavior. Or did she know and just didn't care? He willed himself to calm down enough to ask: "Why did you come here, Mrs. Flanagan? What is it that you think I can do for you?"

His tone was probably a little too harsh for a therapist's office, but judging by her reaction he seemed to have gotten away with it.

"Well," she answered, flustered, now crossing her legs so that her knees pointed towards him, playing with her hair—was she flirting with him?—"last week the website I was registered on, the site that has all the details of my affairs, was hacked."

Robert had heard about that. It had been on the news. The betrayed child within him roared: Good! The cheating bitch is going to get what's coming to her!

He held his breath and nodded, afraid to open his mouth.

"The hackers are threatening to release everyone's information, and...."

Robert snapped. A low cackle escaped his lips. Before he knew it, laughter began to bellow from the pit of his stomach. It was a righteous laugh, a moment of pure condescension.

Debra was taken aback, flustered.

"What is the matter with you, Mr. Davis? Why are you laughing?"

"Because," Robert said, catching his breath, staring at her patronizingly, "it is poetic justice, Mrs. Flanagan. You thought you could have an affair, feel alive, have a little fun, without your actions having any consequences. But now you are afraid that your husband will find out. You are petrified by the idea that your kids will know what kind of woman you really are. You are afraid that you will lose your family because of your indiscretions."

"Yes, of course, I am scared of losing them. This is no laughing matter, Mr. Davis. I came here to get advice on what to do, not to be judged and laughed at," Debra responded, clearly angered by the turn of events.

"Well, too bad, so sad. I don't help cheaters," Robert replied, displaying distinct contempt in his voice. "You walked through the wrong door in search of a sympathetic ear lady. You made your bed—now you are most likely going to be kicked out of it."

What the hell are you doing, the reasonable voice in Robert's head screamed.

None of your business, the emotionally scarred child responded.

Robert was in internal free fall. He felt like he had accidently engaged self-destruct mode—he just couldn't help himself.

Debra arose swiftly and grabbed her Gucci bag, her anger seething.

"You are an absolute ass! If you breathe a word about this to anyone, I will have your therapy license," she shouted while adjusting her dress and storming towards the door. When there, she stopped, turned, and looked him directly in the eyes. "And don't expect to get many clients from here on out Mr. Davis. I will use my connections to destroy you. You are finished. Finished, I tell you." With the force of a tornado, Debra turned on a dime, rushed out, and slammed the door.

"I hope your life falls apart you cheating bitch!" Robert shouted at the top of his lungs.

The room went dead quiet. All he could hear was the sound of her heels clicking as she walked towards her car in the parking lot.

Shit!

Shit, shit, shit, shit, shit!

What have I done?

Chapter 30

Robert went straight to bed when he came home and didn't come out of his room to eat dinner. He barely managed to say goodnight to the kids after Jessica had gotten them ready for bed. When Jessica finally approached him after the kids were asleep, he just lay there, eyes wide open, staring at the ceiling, watching the fan slowly turn round and round.

"What's wrong?" Jessica asked. She sounded genuinely worried.

"I messed up," Robert replied.

"How so?"

Robert didn't answer.

"What's going on Robert? Are you sick? Did something happen at work? Talk to me."

"You would never cheat on me, would you?" Robert finally asked as he made eye contact with her for the first time since he got home.

"Not this again Robert," Jessica answered, "we have gone through this before. I know that I am going on a trip next week, but I thought we had an understanding. Why is this coming up now? Why are you in bed?"

"People cheat, you know," Robert said in a bitter voice. "They say it has nothing to do with love, nothing to do with the other person, but they cheat—mess everything up. They don't realize that it does have something to do with the other person. It does affect them. It hurts, and not just spouses, but also innocents, children. It hurts."

"Where is this coming from, Robert? Why are you acting like this now?" Jessica asked, looking both irritated and fatigued.

"You say you would never cheat, Jessica," Robert said, sitting up, "but you are a textbook case. Your life is monotonous, your relationship with me has very little passion—all we do is divide chores, eat candy and watch TV—and you travel. You have every opportunity to experience adventure every now and then. Are you telling me that you have never even thought about cheating?"

"Yes, Robert. That is what I am telling you. Now stop this. You have no reason to act so suspiciously. I haven't done anything. In fact, I have bent over backward to accommodate you today. I picked up the kids, cooked dinner, got the kids ready for bed, and all while working. You haven't even asked me how my day was. It was horrible. There were layoffs at work and I am supposed to increase sales by twenty percent. But I didn't complain when you came home and went straight to bed. Rather, I tried to make it so that you didn't have to do anything. And this is how you reward me, by accusing me of cheating. Well, I won't be a part of it. I am going to grab some tea and watch TV. You can join me if you like."

She got ready to leave the room, apparently hoping that she had put an end to his jealous inquisition, but he didn't stop. No. He had to push it.

"You're lying, Jessica. I can see it. I can feel it. You have thought about cheating on your trips, haven't you?"

Robert stood up and followed her to the door.

"Admit it, Jessica. You have the same cheating thoughts as everyone else."

He was breathing down her neck, heaving. The animosity was palpable.

"That's enough," Jessica replied. She turned around, looked Robert straight in the eye and whispered menacingly. "I will not be treated this way. You want a confession? You want me to tell you what I have been thinking? Okay then. You win. My answer is yes, I have thought about it. Is that what you want to hear? But so what, I haven't done anyth…"

"Hah! I knew it," Robert roared as he threw his arms into the air. "I knew it. You have thought about cheating. You admit it. Then you have probably flirted, probably signed up for one of those cheating websites. I am guessing that you're just one step away from going through with it. I knew it!"

Robert's brow was heavy. His eyes tried to pierce her soul. There was anger, righteousness, and triumph in his voice. His fists were clenched and his face was red.

"I knew that this relationship, our pact, was too good to be true," Robert roared, doubling down. "You're a cheater, like most of the men and women out there, only thinking of your own pleasure, your own feelings, not minding who you hurt along the way. Cheater. If you haven't done it already, you will soon enough."

"You are an absolute idiot, Robert Davis. I haven't done anything. Nothing I tell you. I work for this family, work for you, you ungrateful son of a bitch, so that you can fulfill your dream. Yes, I have thought about cheating, just like you have thought about it, like both of us have thought about drinking, smoking again, or something equally ridiculous, but I haven't done anything. I kind of wish I had now, since I am being treated like this, but I haven't. Maybe I should cheat, maybe I should have an affair so that your anger will be justified somehow… but I won't."

"You want to have an affair now?" Robert howled as he stormed towards the door. "Well, you've gotta do what you've gotta do. I am not sticking around to be on the receiving end of that. Affairs have caused enough pain in my life. I am leaving."

As he slammed the door, Jessica fell on the bed and started crying.

Chapter 31

Robert was in a delirious state. His heart pumped furiously, his eyes were wide open, he shouted curse words repeatedly at the top of his lungs to the tune of his favorite hard rock radio station, slammed his hands on the steering wheel, shook in his seat, and drove aimlessly around, in a daze. He was a danger to himself and others. He felt pain to the core of his soul.

Alice in Chains was blasting full throttle on the radio, playing *Sickman*. He turned up the volume and screamed at the top of his lungs. He remembered how he and his friends had listened to this song while drinking heavily before they went out on the town in their early twenties. At the time, they said it was a way to get rid of their anger, that they were shouting, neigh, screaming their anger out. Out damn anger, out, they'd said. Yet, every time they followed that script, they would not end up being less angry, no, they would become angrier, and almost without exception, they would end up in a fight.

This was angry music and now, Robert wanted to be angry.

Angry, like when he had broken an antenna off a car in Seattle and then proceeded to scratch every fancy car in sight. Fuck expensive cars and their shiny paint, he'd thought in his righteous teenage rebellion.

Angry, like when he and his friends had nearly beaten a man to death, simply because he was drunk and had bumped into them.

Angry, like when he'd found out that his early twenties girlfriend had cheated on him and he'd threatened to kill her, screaming at the top of his lungs, bitch, bitch, bitch.

Angry, like he had been most of the time before he quit drinking.

Yes, that kind of angry.

Now, sitting in a speeding car, he screamed and thrashed back and forth in his seat.

Aaarrrggghhh!!!

Underneath the pain, he knew he had done everything wrong to-day, from disrespecting his client — and probably ruining his career — to wrongly accusing his wife of cheating, but he wasn't thinking rationally. He was acting emotionally, following a script that he thought he had erased from his databanks. It was the kind of erratic behavior that he hadn't displayed since he lived in Seattle in his late teens. Even his last years of drinking had not been as bad as this. He was witnessing himself going batshit crazy. The reasonable part of his brain was trying to get in edgewise, saying: Stop this madness. You don't have to do this Robert. You can turn around and make it right. It's not too late. But reason didn't have access to the controls.

Was this what a nervous breakdown felt like?

The emotional rollercoaster continued. "Fucking bitches. They all cheat. They all leave. Nobody can be trusted," Robert repeated out loud over and over again.

He was in pain. Not just existential, emotional pain, but physical pain. His nerves were throbbing. His chest felt like it was being ripped in two. He needed relief. Driving around wasn't calming him down. Tears were streaming down his cheeks. His stomach was on fire. He looked at himself in the mirror and hardly recognized the fuming gaze of the madman who was looking back at him. His eyes were openly threatening malfeasance.

You need to calm down Robert, the reasonable voice in his head kept saying.

Fuck you, I won't do what you tell me, Rage Against the Machine screamed on the radio.

Exactly, Robert thought. Fuck you reason. Fuck you. I have tried that. Look where I am at now. In an emotional death spiral.

Pain. Nothing but pain. He needed relief. He needed numbing. He needed a way to get out of his own skin. He needed to escape into an altered state.

At your service, sir. It was the long dormant alcoholic voice within him that spoke. It sounded like a British butler. And what might be the sir's drug of choice tonight?

Robert felt resistance. No. I am not going back there.

Really, sir? You want to feel like this?

Leave me alone. I am not going back. I have too much to lose.

Come now, sir. Could I entice you with some tequila? You used to love tequila. Couldn't get enough of it. We could do shots at a bar. Tequila would have you feeling better in no time.

No.

Ah. Sir is being selective. How about some beer? That would always do the trick, leave you feeling sloshed and sedated at the same time. Wouldn't that be a nice feeling about now? Fill the void in the pit of your stomach and mask the hole in your heart.

I said no!

But, my dear sir. This feeling is no good. How about some Mary Jane? That always used to cheer you up, turn you into a mellow fellow. Smoke a few joints and you'll be feeling alright.

NO!

The car stopped. Robert found himself in the parking lot outside his local Walmart. Hundreds of blackbirds were chirping and cackling, flocking together in the trees, on the power lines, and on top of the building, their incessant noise becoming louder after he turned off the engine and stepped outside. He looked up at the sign. Walmart. It was the superstore for people who wanted to numb their pain. He would find what he needed inside. Robert stumbled towards the building like a zombie who had been starved for brains since the beginning of time.

Once inside, the 24-hour Walmart store looked the same as it always did. High ceilings, bright lights, and gleaming floors welcomed Robert as he walked in. He knew exactly where he was going. The wild-eyed stare on his face must have looked somewhat alarming, at the very least strange, because two employees approached him as he was walking the aisles and asked if he was okay. He nodded and kept going.

Finally, he reached his destination. The candy section.

You must be kidding sir. Candy? That hardly counts as a drug of choice. Come now sir. You can do better than that.

No, Robert said to himself, overriding the pesky alcoholic voice. Candy will do nicely. It has been my drug of choice for twenty years. If I buy enough and eat until I can eat no more, it will dull the pain.

He started rummaging through the shelves and picked out a supersized bag of chocolate covered peanuts, a six-pack of caramel-filled chocolate bars, a box of pecan clusters, and two packs of licorice. He opened the six-pack immediately and devoured a chocolate bar. He felt a little better, but his anger was still seething.

With arms full of candy, Robert made his way towards the register. On the way, he noticed a couple, in their thirties, with three kids—probably between the ages of two and seven—roaming the store.

What the fuck is wrong with people, he thought. It must be after 10 PM on a school night. Keeping the kids up this late borders on child abuse.

He wanted to run up to them, scream at them, get them to change their ways, but instead he put his head down and quickened his step towards the self-serve kiosks. He looked down and noticed that he was wearing his blue, cotton pajama shorts and the white t-shirt he only used for sleeping in. Fuck. I'm in my PJ's. I don't care, he thought angrily. Plenty of people go to the store in their pajamas.

While paying, he downed another chocolate bar and picked up a bottle of soda. He thought about all the times he had been at stores, like this one, late at night and seen people there with their kids. Some people just aren't fit to be parents, he thought. I would never do that to my kids...

A huge lump formed in his throat.

My children.

My family.

What have I done?

A damn of stifled emotions was about to break. He hurried out of the store. As soon as he stepped into the parking lot, he began sobbing uncontrollably in choir with the blackbirds, who were now cackling, chirping and crying louder than ever. Bawling with some restraint, trying not to lose it completely and collapse in the parking lot, Robert hurried to his car, opened the door and slid into the back seat. There, he curled up into the fetal position and let go. He cried as he had never cried before, wailing and shaking, out of self-pity, regret, wallowing in a deep sense of anguish. Tears kept streaming down his cheeks from what seemed like a never-ending well. Little by little, his crying turned into whimpering. As he thought about his wife, he began talking out loud.

"I'm sorry, I'm sorry, I'm sorry. I'm sorry for hurting you, Jessica. I love you. I don't want to lose you. I was angry at my mom, my dad, myself, that redhead bitch that came to my office today. I thought I had forgiven everything. I thought I had worked through it. I'm sorry for losing my shit. I'm sorry for being in such a miserable state. I thought I had more control over my life, my emotions. I'm sorry... "

He tried to calm down his breathing and understand the feelings that were pulsating through him. His previous emotional cocktail of anger and fear was being replaced by utter despair. A black hole of emotional anguish was consuming him.

"Dear Lord," Robert pleaded, to a God he did not believe in, "what am I going to do now?"

He had messed up everything. He had run out on his wife, on his family. What was wrong with him? Where did all of this emotional pain come from? He felt utterly helpless. None of his training had been able to stop him from self-sabotaging.

Finally, the whimpering stopped.

As Robert lay there, in the roomy back seat of his Mercury, he felt drained and exhausted. Despite the noise from the blackbirds—many of whom had now gathered on the top of Robert's car, defecating at their own leisure, underscoring the pile of shit that Robert was in—he was overtaken by a sense of absolute peace. It was internal silence, similar to the kind he had often experienced during meditation, except this time his eyes were wide open. He was depleted. There were no thoughts, no emotions, no stirring in the body. There was only quiet, peace, stillness. It was an eerie feeling, seeing as it had followed the most intense emotional storm Robert had ever weathered in his life, but it was silence nonetheless. A much needed silence. A hiatus from a tidal wave of destructive thoughts and primal fight or flight emotions. Robert was thankful for it. Grateful to get a break.

Alas, the silence did not last for long. Within a few minutes, Robert began thinking about all the damage he had done to his marriage, to his business, to himself. It would take months, even years to rebuild, both internally and externally—that is, if he would be able to rebuild at all. He couldn't figure this out alone. He would need help, but from whom? Who could help him?

Only one person came to his mind.

Robert sat up, rubbed his tear stricken face, climbed into the front seat and started the V6 engine. Roaring to life, it scattered the blackbirds who had gathered on the roof and hood. They left behind an abstract piece of art, white dots on silver.

Robert looked around the parking lot. There were hundreds of blackbirds there, even thousands. They were everywhere. Hitchcock must have gotten the idea for *The Birds* by observing this kind of behavior—seeing thousands of birds flock together for no apparent reason. *The Birds*? Really? Where did that come from? Robert was surprised by the workings of the mind, how easily distracted it was. Here he was, in deep emotional distress, yet he found time to contemplate the origins of a movie that he had never seen.

He opened a bag of chocolate covered peanuts and munched a handful. Looking at his phone, he saw that he had about five missed calls from Jessica plus several texts reading: Are you okay? Where are you? He replied: I am okay. I will be back. Please give me a chance to repair. He took a large swig from his soda, turned on a classical music station, hoping that the music would calm him down, opened one of his licorice bags, and pulled out of the parking lot. The combination of candy and crying was having some effects, slightly numbing the pain, but as he drove towards his destination, Robert felt as low as he had ever felt in his life—lower even than the day he had quit drinking all those years ago. The fifteen-minute drive to his friend's house seemed to take forever.

After he had parked the car, Robert wondered if he should somehow try to improve his appearance, but when he looked into the mirror and saw how puffy and red his eyes were, and noticed the chocolate stain on his white t-shirt, he thought the better of it. Screw it. I am coming here for help. He won't care how I look.

Robert stepped out of the car and walked up the driveway. It was a little after 11 PM when he rang the doorbell. Within a couple of minutes the door opened.

"Jesus, Robert. What happened? What are you doing here?"

"Arthur, I need your help."

Chapter 32

Arthur was a sight for sore eyes, standing in the doorway in a black tank top and checkered pajama pants. Instead of having his usually well-groomed white hair neatly tucked away in a ponytail, it was now unkempt and scruffy, momentarily reminding Robert of Albert Einstein, which brought a slight smile to his face and went against the grain of the painful distortions his facial muscles had been through in the preceding couple of hours. It felt strange and must have looked that way as well; a tortured smile if there ever was one.

"I am sorry to bother you so late Arthur, but I didn't know where else to go," Robert said in a broken voice. His throat felt sore from all the crying he had done.

Arthur responded like Robert had hoped, by inviting him in, showing him into the kitchen and making some herbal tea.

"Okay brother. Let's talk," he said.

Robert didn't need to be asked twice. The words started rolling off his tongue and the soreness in his throat quickly subsided. Within thirty minutes, he had told Arthur everything, about how he had snapped during today's therapy session, how he had dragged those foul emotions into his home, into his relationship, how he had falsely accused Jessica, stormed out and then suffered a total breakdown. Furthermore, he explained how his business was going nowhere, how he constantly doubted his masculinity, and how his interactions with Vigo had confused him.

"You've certainly made a mess," Arthur responded when Robert finally stopped talking.

"I know," Robert said, clasping his head in his hands. "I'm screwed."

"What does that mean to you—being screwed?" Arthur replied.

"It means that I have messed things up beyond repair Arthur. I messed up my marriage, my family life, my business. It's all messed up. I'm screwed," Robert replied in despair, his eyes welling up again.

"I have seen things messed up beyond repair Robert, and your situation does not fit that description," Arthur answered calmly.

"Really?" Robert said, willing to grasp onto any shred of hope.

"Yes. I am not saying that things will go back to the way they were, simply because I don't know how other people will react to what you have done, but your problems are mostly of your own doing, and that you can fix," Arthur explained.

"What do you mean, my problems are mostly of my own doing?" Robert replied.

"What I mean is, that aside from your failing business, which is only partly your fault, you have made every other problem worse by thinking too much, by interpreting, by seeing things that weren't there," Arthur said, leaning back in his chair, taking a sip of his chamomile tea from a colorful cup that had the inscription *Love, Laugh, Live*.

"I can see how some of it was my fault… but I am not willing to admit that it was all my fault," Robert replied, trying to defend what sliver of dignity he had left. Sure, he had messed up, but he wasn't going to take full responsibility for all of it.

"Let's stop for a moment and think about it, shall we?" Arthur said, then continued without waiting for a response. "Right now, at this moment, what is going on?"

"I am spilling my guts here, in severe emotional pain, and you are playing word games, telling me that everything is my fault," Robert answered, halfway regretting his decision to look to Arthur for help.

"My dear brother. That's your interpretation of the situation. Please humor me and answer my question literally. Right now, at this moment, what is going on? Don't interpret."

"Right now, I am sitting in your kitchen, talking to you, drinking peppermint tea from a black cup. There. Was that what you were looking for?" Robert replied, now angered. "I have been through these types of exercises before Arthur. I don't think that a be here now exercise is going to cut it."

"Then I dare say that you have missed the point of those exercises. Right now, at this moment, there is no problem," Arthur replied, pausing for effect.

He was right. At that moment, in the kitchen, sitting together, drinking tea, there was no problem. Still, Robert felt rotten, the effects of the emotional tornado he had been through still reverberated through every cell of his being.

"I am not saying that we shouldn't try to work on your problems," Arthur continued, "including your internal angst, and I am not saying that we shouldn't think. All I am saying is that it is important to put things in perspective. Let us, for example, examine your interaction with your client earlier today. As I understand it, what happened was that a woman walked into your office, told you some things, to which you responded, and then she walked out. It was your response that created the problem, your memories, your interpretation of the situation, not the situation itself. Wouldn't you agree?'

"Yes, but those interpretations are part of my psychological makeup, a part that I thought I had dealt with. I was sure that events from my childhood would never bother me again. I thought I had forgiven everything. Yet, the memories and emotions crept up on me, ambushed me from out of nowhere. All of a sudden I was completely out of control," Robert replied, his voice breaking.

"Exactly. You were out of control. You. Not the situation," Arthur said. "The same thing happened when you met your wife tonight. She was minding her own business, did nothing to provoke you, and you decided to blow things up. You. That is my point. You created these problems, which means that you can fix them."

"I used to believe that Arthur," Robert replied, still feeling emotionally raw. "I used to think that if problems were internal, then they could be fixed, that if my thoughts and emotions were the root causes, then I had complete control over them. But, I realize now that not everything can be changed."

He paused and a terrible thought occurred to him.

"Maybe my deep seeded mistrust is a subconscious emotional trigger that I will never be able to get rid of."

Arthur did not respond, rather listened intently as he took a sip of his tea.

"To be honest with you," Robert continued, flustered by his realization, "I thought I was out of the woods. Sure, I knew I was still flawed, but I never expected this kind of internal explosion. I mean, if you could see the amount of work I have put in—the therapy, the AA meetings, the number of books I have read, the hours I have spent on my meditation cushions, the continuous introspection, the be here now approach—all in an effort to change, to reduce the destructive effects of my childhood, then you would understand why I was so surprised by what transpired today."

Robert was truly and sincerely baffled. How had it come to this? During his twenty years of sobriety, fifteen years of marriage, and ten years of parenting, he had never lost control like he had done today.

"I once heard a story about the marketing director of Coca-Cola," Arthur said, seemingly swerving off topic. "He was flying across the Atlantic, first class. When his traveling companion found out what he did, he asked: Why does Coca-Cola advertise so much? Your products sell whether you market them or not. The marketing director responded: You wouldn't want the pilot to stop flying the plane midway over the Atlantic would you? We advertise for the same reason. When something works, we keep doing it. We don't stop flying midair."

Robert knew that he had just been on the receiving end of an NLP trick—the telling of a seemingly unrelated story to jar the client. It got to him nonetheless.

Had he stopped flying midair? He rapidly went over his checklist. Going to AA meetings? Nope, he hadn't done that since September. Reading something inspiring? No, not for a long time. Exercising? Not at all, as was evident by his flabbiness. Journaling and making emotional checklists? No, he hadn't engaged in that for a while. Meditation? No, he'd allowed Vigo to screw that up for him.

In essence, he had done none of the things that had kept him sober and functioning for the past twenty years. None of the little things that had kept him from relapsing, not just from drinking again, but from going into the kind of emotional tailspin that usually lead to drinking — the kind that he had just experienced. Tonight, he could've easily ended up in a bar. In fact, it would have been the rational response to his emotional distress, to numb the pain with something stronger than candy.

He looked at Arthur, grateful for having shown up on his doorstep, and said: "I guess I did stop flying midair."

Arthur looked pleased when he saw Robert's moment of realization and asked: "What are you going to do about it, brother?"

"I guess I'd better get back to flying," Robert replied, smiling slightly, as he saw the path laid out before him. He would need to get back into rhythm, clean up his own act, and then fix whatever could be fixed. He needed to get back to his regular meetings, his walking routine, his emotional checklist, counting his blessings, and most importantly, back to meditating. Could he?

"I don't know if meditation can be part of my routine again Arthur," Robert said.

"Why not?" Arthur asked.

"Because it scares me. My interactions with Vigo sucked me into some kind of philosophical vortex. I can't get back to thinking about meditation as my moments of peace. Now, meditation seems emblematic of some sort of anti-life agenda — about somehow turning away from everything that is most dear to me and embracing a part of myself that I would rather not identify with too strongly," Robert replied hesitantly.

"Correct me if I am wrong brother, but meditation has been an important part of your sobriety, right?"

"Yes," Robert replied. "It has been my way to reset emotions, to regain equilibrium."

"Then you have to redefine your relationship with meditation Robert. You can't discard it, any more than a pilot can discard the fuel for his engine."

"But how?"

There was a short silence while the two of them pondered the question. Finally, Arthur leaned back in his chair and asked: "What is the most important thing in your life?"

"My family," Robert answered without delay.

"Which means that your answer is love," Arthur replied.

"I guess," Robert responded.

"Then love must be the new element around which your meditation practice revolves," Arthur stated ceremoniously, his deep voice as convincing as ever.

Love? The rational part of Robert's brain wasn't entirely happy with getting the fortune cookie result of, love is the answer, yet he had to entertain the idea, if for no other reason than the severity of his situation. What he had been doing had resulted in a mental and emotional breakdown. Maybe it was time to try something slightly different.

"How would I do that exactly?" Robert asked, feeling vulnerable, open to suggestion. "How would I include the element of love in my meditation?"

"Well, you would need to build on feelings of genuine love, for example, the love you feel for your family," Arthur replied. "Furthermore, as you have pointed out, maybe you need to embrace a complete philosophy in relation to your meditation practice, one that embraces the concept of love. Having been brought up in a Christian environment, you might want to look there for inspiration."

Hell no, was Robert's internal response, I'm not that vulnerable. Don't tell me to look for solace in the Bible.

"With all due respect Arthur, I am not ready to embrace a mythic belief system just because I am feeling emotionally distraught," Robert replied.

"I am not saying that you should become a born again Christian, brother, but you have to admit that love and compassion are values that are at the heart of what Jesus taught, evident by quotes such as, *Turn the other cheek*, *You are the light of the world*, and *Love thy neighbor as thyself*. If you read the New Testament from that perspective, with love, grace, and compassion as the essential elements around which

143

all else is built, then I bet that even you could begin to see God in a new light," Arthur replied.

"Look, Arthur, I am shaken, but not stirred," Robert said, glad to hear that he was regaining his simplistic pun based sense of humor. "I am willing to include love in my practice, sure, but I'm not ready to embrace ideas about an all-powerful God that somehow has an interest in my personal life, an absent father in heaven if you will. I already have one of those. Honestly, I don't see how reverting to my Christian roots will help me piece my life back together."

"Understood brother. I was as jaded as you are once. It took a long time for me to reconnect with my roots, even after I joined Unity. But after I did, after I saw the power of believing in love and compassion, I somehow felt whole again. That was the only reason why I suggested it," Arthur explained. "All I ask is that you don't close the door on it completely."

Robert nodded hesitantly, even though he knew that the God door had been welded shut for a long time.

"Tomorrow, I suggest that you try meditating with me, using a loving visualization," Arthur said as he stepped away from the table and put both of their mugs in the sink.

"Yeah, I'd like that," Robert replied.

He was exhausted. It was already passed midnight.

When Robert had arrived, Arthur had told him to text Jessica, to let her know where he would be spending the night. Then Arthur had called her to calm her down.

Arthur was a good friend.

Chapter 33

"Up and at'em brother."

Robert turned around on the brown leather sofa he had slept in and saw Arthur standing over him, smiling broadly and looking like he had already exercised and taken a shower.

What time was it?

Robert looked at the living room clock. It was 6.30 AM. He felt rotten. His teeth felt wooly, his eyes were swollen—so much so that he had difficulty keeping them open—and his head throbbed incessantly like he had been drinking the previous night.

Boy, am I glad I didn't choose that route, he reasoned.

As he tried to sit up, his back ached from sleeping in the same position for the couple of hours he had slept. After Arthur had gone to bed the previous night, Robert had laid awake on the sofa, trying to figure out how he was going to fix the mess that he had made.

First, he'd have to come clean with Jessica, tell her everything and hope that she would forgive him. They had been through some bumpy times, but his behavior last night had created the biggest obstacle to their future together yet.

Second, he would need to whip himself into shape again, mentally, emotionally, physically. He needed to get back to the basics. His regular twelve step meetings seemed like the logical place to start. AA had always been there for him and even though he hadn't ended up in a bar last night, it had been the closest he had ever been to falling off the wagon since he quit drinking. Meeting with the Council more regularly also seemed prudent. It was clear that he wasn't thinking straight and he would need to borrow wisdom, at the very least mirror his ideas. Maybe it was even time that he started seeing a therapist of his own, something he had been urged to do ever since he started his education in the field. He'd seen plenty of therapists before starting his education but had somehow felt that being a therapist himself meant that he had graduated, that he didn't need one. Maybe that was his central problem.

Third? He didn't really know what else to do. Arthur had rightly pointed out that he couldn't figure everything out in advance. Living life from moment to moment, while figuring out what ideas were helping and which ones were hurting, seemed like the right thing to do.

That was it.

Third, live moment to moment. Don't make any rash decisions.

A deep feeling of sorrow had swept over Robert when he'd thought about the possibility that Jessica might not be willing to put up with his emotional instability and jealousy anymore, that she might not want to live with him. He couldn't imagine life without her and the kids. An intense sense of loneliness had enveloped him when he entertained the thought of losing his family—even as he had just made a decision to live in the moment. The mind was a fickle creature. He had wept himself to sleep on the sofa. Was the well of tears endless?

"Meet me in my bedroom in ten minutes," Arthur said in a commanding tone.

Oh, yes, Robert realized. It's morning. The two of us are going to meditate together.

Robert hurried to the bathroom, washed his face and put some of Arthur's toothpaste on his finger, smearing it on his teeth. He even managed to swallow half a cup of coffee before he entered Arthur's bedroom. It was the first time he had been in there. The large room was bare. There was a twin bed in one corner, a small altar to Arthur's deceased wife in another corner, and a large picture frame on the central wall, with what seemed to be a tie-dye or splash-like orange artwork that had a small hole in the middle and light shining through it from the back. Arthur had placed two meditation cushions on the floor in front the picture.

"Sit here," Arthur motioned to the purple cushion beside him, adding, "this, on the wall, is a mandala," he said, pointing to the picture. "We will use it as our point of reference as we meditate."

"Okay," Robert replied, as he tried to cross his legs and straighten his back. His body was not cooperating. In addition to not being used to meditate in the mornings, his worn out muscles were stiff and tender. He ached all over. Under normal circumstances, he would have excused himself, but Robert knew that he needed a new approach to his meditation practice if he were to revive it.

"I am going to have you try a simple visualization process," Arthur explained. "First, narrow your eyelids to a sliver and focus on the light emanating from the mandala. Second, use the word light as you inhale. Imagine that you are inhaling pure, golden light through your forehead. Third, use the word love as you exhale and imagine that the light you inhaled through your forehead is traveling down to your heart and transforming it into a well of luminosity. See your heart expanding as the well fills up. From then on, continue this same process. Inhale light and exhale love. Imagine your head being filled with light and your heart being filled with love."

Robert nodded. He wasn't sure about this approach. He had purposely avoided any form of visualization since he began his meditation practice. In his workshops, he had often likened visualization to playing movies in the mind. Even now, his rational mind sowed seeds of doubt, telling him that this process wouldn't work, but when Robert focused on his heart, it felt like an open wound, raw, sensitive, and tender, like it had been torn, twisted and trampled. Overriding his rationality, he surrendered to his need for healing and submitted to the process.

Through the sliver between his eyelids, the light emanating from the hole in the orange picture shone like the rays of the sun.

Inhale light.

Robert felt a sensation materialize on the center of his forehead. It felt like a tickling or pulsing sensation between his eyebrows.

Exhale love.

As he tried to visualize the light going into his heart, Robert felt the area tighten up and a lump formed in his throat, like he was about to weep again.

Surrender to the process, he thought, heal the heart.

He deepened his breathing, relaxing more with every inhalation and exhalation. The lump slowly dissolved.

Inhale light. Relax.

Exhale love. Relax.

Feeling love in his heart was harder than Robert had expected. The rhythmic pulsing sensation in his forehead continued, and yet his heart felt locked, closed, dark. Nevertheless, he continued with the process.

Inhale light. Relax.

Exhale love. Relax.

Breath by breath his heart softened.

Finally, light was allowed to enter through a small crack. Once the light was in, Robert's mind was flooded with images of himself as a child — lost, scared, alone.

Hello, little Robbie. Why are you so scared? Where are your mommy and daddy? Robert picked little Robbie up, rocking him gently back and forth, calming his fears, easing his loneliness. It's okay little Robbie. Shhh. It's okay.

Inhale light.

Exhale love.

More images swarmed Robert's mind. Scenes of his mom and dad arguing, from the time he was a baby to just before his father passed away. He saw a cascade of pictures of all the women he had hurt, both intentionally and unintentionally since he first started dating. Their faces were tortured when he took away the promise of love. Bad Robbie. Hurtful Robbie.

He tried to remain focused on light and love. Another emotion came to mind. Forgive Robbie. Really? For all that? Yes, forgive Robbie.

Inhale light.

Exhale love.

He saw calming images of his wife, Jessica. Of her talking sweetly to him, stroking his hair, looking deeply into his eyes as they made love. She was his rock, the love of his life. He saw scenes of their wedding day. How beautiful she looked in her golden and white wedding dress. How her smile had never been brighter. He saw images of her giving birth to their children, red, sweaty, in pain, crying and smiling as they were put on her breast—never more beautiful. Images of James and Cathy followed, laughing and crying in his arms, snuggling close to him in bed, singing together in the mornings, walking cheerfully home from school. His eyes welled up once again. The love he felt for the three of them was tangible, palpable, powerful. Now, the light he experienced was golden, warm, thick, comforting, consoling. It was love like he had never felt it before.

Inhale light.

Exhale love.

What followed was a never-ending onslaught of comforting images and emotions. In some sense, it should have felt overwhelming, but the comfort was so pleasant, that it never became too intense.

After what seemed like an eternity, the images stopped and were replaced with peace. Everything else dropped away and only peace remained, healing and calming, different from the other times he had experienced it. He surrendered and allowed himself to be completely immersed.

Silence.

Silence.

Silence.

Peace.

Twenty-five minutes after they'd begun, Robert's awareness was pulled back into the moment when Arthur banged a small gong that he had underneath the mandala. Gong. Gong. Gong. Then Arthur chanted, Om Shanti, peace, three times, and added, In the name of the Father, the Son, and the Holy Spirit, crossing himself, as Robert gradually opened his eyes.

"How do you feel brother?" Arthur asked in his deep voice, creating its signature pacifying effect on Robert.

"I feel well. Better than I've felt in a long time," Robert confessed. He wasn't bothered by the stiffness in his body anymore. It felt like his entire being had been recharged in some mysterious way.

"Good. I am glad to hear that brother."

"It was quite an experience, like a catharsis of sorts, an emotional cleansing," Robert explained. "All kinds of emotions and images went through my mind as I made an effort to fill my heart with light and love."

Arthur nodded.

"And then I felt absolute peace, different from what I've felt before. Not like there was nothing... but rather a sense of comfort, warmth, hope, and healing," Robert added, "but it was peace, similar to the peace I have felt numerous times before, only the texture had changed. How do you explain that?"

"My dearest brother," Arthur said, looking deeply into Robert's eyes, "I have never disagreed with you about the fact that there is peace during meditation. I have just disagreed with you about what it meant. By surrounding your practice with light and love, you have changed the feeling of the peace. It is no longer an abyss. It is no longer emptiness. It is exactly how you described it, comforting and healing."

Tears came to Robert's eyes as he listened.

"Yes," he replied. "Comforting and healing."

"Let me promise you this, my brother. As long as you summon the energies of light and love during your practice, you will never get lost. You will always find your way back to the light."

Chapter 34

It was almost 9.30 AM when Robert arrived at his home. The Halloween decorations that he had put out the previous weekend adorned the front porch, consisting of a couple of witches, the obligatory fake spider web, and a lit pumpkin, which Jessica had forgotten to turn off that morning—who could blame her?

Arthur had called Jessica after the men had finished their morning meditation. During the phone call, he had learned that she had taken the day off from work and was at home waiting for Robert. The kids were already at school. The couple would have the whole day to themselves.

Be open and honest with her, Arthur had told Robert as they had parted ways that morning. Stay in the light, be vulnerable, and you will be alright. I could hear it in her voice, he'd added, she wants to forgive you.

Robert parked the car in front of the garage, turned off the engine and got ready to get out. He looked down at the clothes he was wearing, a tie-dye shirt and light brown hemp shorts, both of which he had borrowed from Arthur's closet.

Should I have worn something else? Stopped at Target on my way home? I couldn't very well wear the stained pajamas I left the house in last night. Will what I am wearing have an effect on the way that she greets me?

Get it together Robert. Breathe. Breathe.

What would I do without the calm and reasonable voice in my head?

After ten deep breaths, he shook his head, drummed quickly on the steering wheel, opened the car door and got out. Walking away from the car, he locked it with his clicker. The beep as the doors locked sounded louder than usual and startled him. He was wound up. A bundle of nerves. The bad kind of primed. Stressed and anxious. With every step he took towards his house he tried to calm himself, mentally repeating the words he had learned that morning. Inhale light. Exhale love.

He opened the door gently, like a burglar in the night. As he peeked inside, he called, "Jessica?"

"In here," she replied, the sound coming from the kitchen.

He couldn't read anything into her tone. Was she mad or sad? Both? Neither? Neither would be worst. He could take anger and sadness, but not apathy. He had often felt indifference from his parents, like they didn't care about him or his brother, like they only cared about themselves. That had hurt him more than any display of anger. Not caring would be the worst response.

Don't drag all that shit in with you Robert. Be in the moment.

The reasonable voice in his head now sounded like Arthur.

He walked into the kitchen, where Jessica stood by the sink, looking out the window.

"Hey you," Robert said, ever so gently.

Jessica turned around, her eyes puffy and red. She'd been crying.

She did care! What a relief!

"Hey," she replied.

Robert didn't know what to do or say, so he did the only thing he knew how to in the situation. He walked towards her with open arms, hoping for a hug. Jessica didn't respond immediately, but as he got closer, she hesitantly raised her arms and hugged him, first semi-angrily, hammering his back, exclaiming, you idiot, a few times and then finally settling into a warm embrace.

As they hugged — her head nestled in his neck — Robert felt a sense of relief accompanied by a sense of sorrow. How had he let it get this far? A whirlwind of emotions swept through him as they stood there hugging. He didn't know what she was thinking, but the hug signified a willingness to work things out. At the very least, the physical contact was lessening the knot in his stomach and the tightness around his heart. When they finally let go of each other, Jessica looked him in the eyes and said firmly: "Now. You need to tell me everything, Robert Davis. Everything."

They sat down at the kitchen table and for the second time in twelve hours Robert recounted everything that had happened—except this time it didn't take thirty minutes, more like an hour and a half.

He told her about his failing business; how he felt like less of a man for not being able to contribute to the household; how he'd felt compelled to keep it from her, somehow thinking that it would be better if he figured it out on his own.

He told her about Dr. Vigo Andersen; how he'd been back to see the doctor even if he knew he was in over his head. How their interactions had messed with his head, his ideas about life and death, and his meditation practice, which was why he had stopped meditating. Then he told her how Arthur had suggested a new approach, centered on love.

She smiled when she heard that.

He told her how he had isolated himself in the past month; how he had not been to a single AA meeting; how he had not met anyone from the Council until he showed up at Arthur's doorstep last night.

He told her about all his fears; how he wanted them to be a family more than anything; how he was afraid that his jealousy would destroy their marriage; how the cheating woman who had come to his office yesterday had somehow been the straw that broke the camel's back, sending him into an emotional frenzy—one that he had brought home with him last night.

In between, he repeatedly pleaded with her to forgive him. He promised to be more forthright from now on, to start doing the little things that kept him sane—sincerely adding that he wanted to guarantee that this would never happen again, but that he couldn't say anything concrete, seeing how broken he really was.

All the while, Jessica just sat there and listened. She didn't say much, but rather nodded her head and used Robert's trick of saying, go on, whenever he paused for a moment. When he was done, she was smiling ever so slightly, like she was somehow relieved.

"Why are you smiling?" Robert asked, not knowing what to expect.

"I don't know," she replied. "I just thought it would be much worse."

Worse? How could it be worse, Robert thought.

"How so?"

"Well, I thought you might have been cheating on me, deep in debt, or worse, that you might have started drinking again."

She paused. Robert held his breath.

"But this, what you just told me, is just the same old stuff that I have known about for years. I have known that you had trust issues for a long time and I've made my peace with that. I have known that you want to be the man of the house, whatever that means, and we can figure that out. And Robert, my love, I knew that your business was in the crapper, I just didn't want to say anything. The only two things I am extremely unhappy about are, number one that you lied to me—don't ever do that again, our relationship is based on honesty and so is your sobriety—and number two, how you acted last night, which was unacceptable. Granted, you seem to have experienced an emotional breakdown—which explains a lot of things—but truth be told, I don't know if I can handle many of those."

Again, she paused.

"Now, I am willing to forgive you on two conditions. One, that you never lie to me again, and two, that you keep doing whatever it was that prevented you from having such a breakdown in the past fifteen years of our marriage. Can you do that?"

Robert was stunned. Jessica was so calm and collected about the whole thing. He couldn't believe it. Yes. Yes. Yes. He wanted to jump for joy. He thought he'd lost her. He thought he'd be barred from seeing his kids except every other weekend. He thought…

Not wasting a moment, he leaped on her suggestions, telling her that he was already planning to get back into his routine, that he was finally going to start seeing a therapist in order to figure out ways to prevent this from happening again, and that he would never lie to her again, no matter what. As she tentatively accepted his apology, they embraced again, this time with less uncertainty.

What relief. He melted into her embrace. It felt like the tension that had been building up for weeks was being drained. He knew that he still had a lot of work to do, that he still had to prove himself, but she had forgiven him—at least in word. Their relationship would need mending, it would take time, but that was okay. He had time. Especially if he was with her. With them. His family.

Jessica and Robert went into the living room and cuddled together in the corner of the sofa.

"I owe you an apology as well," Jessica said hesitantly after they settled down.

"No. Absolutely not. This was all on me," Robert answered.

"No, I do Robert, and you know it," she replied. "I was emotionally unstable last night and could have managed the situation a lot better. I knew you were in pain, but I just couldn't handle the accusations. That's why I blew up. I am sorry about that."

"You have nothing to be sorry about. I was the one who fell apart," he said.

"Accept my apology anyway," she said, as she hugged him tightly.

"Okay."

For a while, they just sat there in silence, looking around the living room, the family pictures, the bookshelves filled with psychology literature, the ceiling fan that rotated above them ever so slowly, and they repeatedly looked at each other to confirm that everything was okay. Robert stroked Jessica's hair and held her tightly, while Sandy lay by their feet, snoring and whimpering, evidently dreaming a doggy dream.

"You know what?" Jessica finally said, breaking the silence.

"What?" Robert replied in a dazed tone. He was exhausted.

"I read this great article about relationships last night when I was researching how to handle what had just happened. The article compared people to stained glass windows. It said that when a window had been broken, it could never be put together in the same way again. That the vulnerabilities, the cracks in the glass would always show."

"That's doesn't sound very encouraging," Robert said, sitting up slightly.

"No, there was more," she added quickly. "The moral of the analogy was that no matter how badly a stained glass window has been broken, if put back together, it will still provide beautiful light when the sun shines through it. That's a lovely thought, don't you think?"

"Yes. That is lovely," he responded.

He was just happy to be home.

"I took the light to mean love," Jessica continued. "Both of us are like broken stained glass windows Robert—you because of your cheating parents and me because of my alcoholic dad—but, when we allow love to shine through, we produce a wonderful rainbow of lights."

"You are saying that it's better to be broken together than it is to be broken apart?" Robert said with a slight chuckle. "See what I did there, broken apart?"

"You moron," Jessica replied, laughing.

Yes. He made her laugh.

He was going to do much more of that.

Chapter 35

One week after patching things up with Jessica, Robert was at his favorite Starbucks inside the Barnes & Noble store at the Arboretum. Things had been better since he'd confessed, vowed to get back into his routine, and swore never to lie to her again. To his amazement, James and Cathy seemed oblivious to what had happened, which was a testament to how much of Robert's crisis had been in his own head. His primary goal of providing his children with an upbringing they didn't have to recover from—free from alcoholism, abuse, extramarital affairs, and divorce—was still on its way to being realized.

During the week that had passed, he'd gone the extra mile to make sure they were alright, reading to his little princess every night and spending extra time with his son when he tucked him in. The kids seemed alright. Better than that actually. Their lives had continued like nothing had ever happened, except for the fact that daddy had been gone one night.

Robert had also made an extra effort with Jessica. Snuggling with her in the evenings, instead of them sitting on opposite ends of the sofa, whispering sweet nothings in her ear, and showing her that he was recovering from his state of inner turmoil by resuming his meditation practice, this time focusing on love and light. She'd responded well, evident by the number of loving glances and warm embraces they had exchanged over the course of the week.

To show that he was moving expeditiously, Robert had even met with his new therapist, Ellie Goldberg, who was one of his teachers from college. She had recently opened a private practice in Round Rock. Although it had only been their first session, both of them realized that much work needed to be done, especially concerning his childhood.

I thought I'd forgiven my parents already, he'd blurted out during their first session, to which she replied that forgiveness, like love, was a commitment that needed to be renewed on a regular basis.

Robert had also gone to a couple of AA meetings and was scheduled to meet the Council on the weekend. Small steps, he thought to himself. Baby steps. No rash actions.

Nonetheless, one giant decision was staring him in the face. It was a decision that he wished he didn't have to make during this time of emotional vulnerability. Yet, the more he thought about it, the more he realized that he couldn't hold it off any longer. It concerned his therapy practice. It was evident to him that he couldn't afford to keep it. However hard it would be, he had to close it down. His lease expired in December, so it was a good time to make this decision for practical reasons, but it would be difficult nonetheless. He had invested so much of his life into that business—his heart, his soul, his time, his money. Closing it would be painful. He'd have to approach it like he was ripping off a bandage—devote one day to contacting his clients, letting the landlord know that he wasn't going to renew his lease, close his bank accounts, etc. Yep, he would just have to rip it off.

Be grateful, the reasonable, Arthuresque voice in his head said. Considering what a mess you made, you only have to let go of your practice. You're lucky.

He didn't feel lucky, though. He felt like he was killing off a part of himself, similar to what the Buddhist monk Daigen had described. He was dying to a separate part of himself—killing off the therapist who ran his own private practice. Robert knew that there were plenty of identities roaming around in his head that could replace that character, but sending the private practice therapist to his death wouldn't be easy.

Robert stood up to get a refill on his coffee. As he was pouring the black liquid into his cup, he felt a tap on his shoulder. When he turned around, he had to do a double-take to recognize the man standing before him. It was a scruffy looking Bill—an AA acquaintance from ten years ago when Robert first came to Austin. They had met each other from time to time in meetings over the years and always told each other how things were going. For fun, they would jokingly say, to anyone that passed them, that they were Bill and Bob, referring to the two founders of the twelve step program, usually eliciting a smile, sometimes a laugh. Now, Robert put his coffee cup down and the two men hugged, thumping each other robustly on the back in a manly sort of way. As he stepped back to look at Bill, Robert noticed how much he had aged since the last time they saw each other and how poorly he looked. He was wearing what could only be described as tattered clothing, a bluish American Eagle t-shirt, frayed khaki shorts, and blue Crocs that were close to being worn through.

"Robert. Bob. Bobbie," Bill said, as they stood there looking at each other, "it's good to see you, man. Been awhile."

"Yeah, it has. Too long. How's it going, my friend?" Robert asked.

"I fucked up man. I have only been sober for a month now," Bill replied like he had been waiting for an opportunity to blurt it out.

"What? How?" Robert responded incredulously. "I mean, the last time I saw you everything was going so well. You were celebrating fifteen years of sobriety. What happened?"

They sat down for a mini-meeting of which Robert had conducted many during his years of sobriety. He urged Bill to tell him everything. He wasn't going anywhere. He had time to listen.

"I don't know man. It started innocently enough. I guess it was just one thing that led to another," Bill explained, as he hung his head. "I stopped going to meetings, stopped meditating, stopped praying, stopped doing all the things that I'd been doing to stay sober. Then things just started sliding, you know man. I started smoking tobacco again, let down my guard. I didn't remember how closely knit smoking and drinking had been. Because I wasn't going to meetings, I stopped hanging around sober people and started hanging around my friends from work. They seemed to be having so much fun man. At a company barbecue this spring I had a couple of beers. Nothing happened the next day, so I thought I could handle it, declared that I was no longer an alcoholic. It worked for a couple of months, during which I went to the company poker games, smoked cigars, drank whiskey and beer, and went to work the next day. I believed that I was cured."

Robert realized that Bill had jeopardized everything that he had worked for over the years, including his family—a wife and two young daughters.

"Then, pretty soon, everything took a turn for the worse," Bill said with sadness in his voice. "I got into a gambling debt that I couldn't pay straight away. I lied to my wife about it. Then somebody at work suggested that we go to Vegas. Shit yeah man, I said, then I can win back my debt. Of course, I didn't. Rather I started taking cocaine to stay awake while I was there and got deeper into debt. One thing lead to another and before you knew it I was dealing drugs on the side to pay my debts, that is, until my boss found out about it and fired me. He even called my wife. Can you believe that man?"

Yes I can, Robert thought to himself, but he said nothing, just nodded his head sympathetically.

"I was furious man. Me and my wife had a huge fight and she left with the girls. She's been staying with her mom since July. I thought that her leaving would be enough to get me straightened out, but I just kept at it, you know. Then, the house turned into a pigsty when my dealer moved in with me. It was horrible. Soon after that, we were busted."

"No way," Robert replied in disbelief.

"Yes way," Bill replied remorsefully. "I was sentenced to treatment and community service, you know, because it was my first offense. I'm just lucky I didn't get caught back in the day. Now, I am living in a halfway house, the wife and girls are back in our house, but she wants a divorce."

Robert must have looked stunned as they sat there in silence.

"I told you, man. I fucked up royally."

"You can say that again," Robert replied. "How are you doing now?"

"I'm surviving, you know. One day at a time. Ready to surrender to the fact that I am an alcoholic. Still on the first step, though. I tell you. It hurts. From almost fifteen years of sobriety to this, it's a long way to fall," Bill replied.

Yes, a long way, Robert thought. A very long way.

After talking for a while longer, the two men exchanged phone numbers and Robert suggested that they meet for coffee after their regular AA meeting on the weekend. Bill agreed and they hugged again, this time holding a little tighter as if to say that everything would be okay.

Walking to his car, Robert compared what he had just heard to his own situation. He had a reason to be grateful. Things could have turned out much worse.

Chapter 36

It was the day before Thanksgiving break and both kids had awards ceremonies at school. They were quick to get up and get ready. Robert enjoyed every moment of that morning; singing his favorite tune, *Good Morning* from *Singin' in the Rain*, to his kids to wake them up, brushing their teeth, getting Cathy dressed, making lunches with Jessica. Every minute he felt like he was performing a valuable service.

The turnaround was astounding. In the three weeks since his breakdown, Robert's relationship with Jessica had improved steadily with every passing day and his routine had become more stable. At the behest of his therapist, he had tried not to overcompensate for his screw up. If you try to be perfect, she'd told him, then you are setting an impossible standard for yourself in the future.

Why he hadn't started seeing a therapist many years ago was still a mystery. Having a confidant made life a lot easier.

Other than that, he was trying to live life moment to moment, enjoying each one that he got to spend with his family. As the four of them made their way to the elementary school, Robert was skipping and jumping, running around with the kids, teasing Jessica, making jokes and laughing.

"Take it easy Peter Pan," Jessica said with a chuckle when he almost fell over.

She called me Peter Pan, he thought. Wow. What a difference a few weeks can make. She hasn't called me that in years.

At school, Jessica and Robert sat among the other parents on hard plastic chairs in the large echo-chamber of a cafeteria, shifting their weight constantly so their butts wouldn't fall asleep, waiting for the kids to arrive on stage. In years past, Robert had deeply resented coming to these meaningless affairs, but today he was delighted to be here. His family was his community, his main avenue of service. Being a man, at least in the social sense, meant being there for them, no matter what the activity was. Being a man biologically, well, he wasn't too concerned about that anymore. He felt more at peace with his role than he had for years.

Instead of being bent over his phone, like most everyone else, Robert allowed his mind to wander. Ever since he had stayed with Arthur that fateful night a few weeks back—which quite frankly, felt like a lifetime ago—Robert had frequently thought about what love meant to him. He still used the mantra that Arthur had taught him and not only when he meditated, but also when he needed to calm himself down during the day. Inhale light. Exhale love. The Council had agreed to have a special Thanksgiving meeting about love on Black Friday that he was looking forward to. Instead of shopping, they would philosophize. It was a great idea that had come from George of all people. Each of them was to bring a quote about love and then they would talk about their experiences and thoughts on the subject.

As the kids walked on stage, receiving their awards, Robert beamed with pride. Cathy got an award for behavior. James got one for academic progress. He sat there and soaked in the scenery while Jessica ran around with her phone, taking as many pictures as she could. Each of them had their own way of savoring the moment.

After congratulating the kids and taking them back to their classrooms, Robert shared his thoughts with Jessica. Maybe he was going overboard, but these days he just shared everything. No secrets.

"Do you think I should go back to see Dr. Andersen at some point?"

"Why would you want to do that?" she replied.

"I don't know? It just seems like I owe him an apology. He was part of my downward spiral after all. I've been apologizing to everyone else who was involved, why not him?"

"Do you think you are strong enough to face him?"

"Yeah, I think so, I mean, he got to me, but I have sorted things out now. I just feel like we parted on unacceptable terms."

"If you think it will make you feel better," Jessica replied, "then by all means do it, but only if you think you are strong enough. I really don't want to go through another breakdown with you just yet, okay?"

"Another breakdown? The way I am feeling now, the probability of me suffering another breakdown is close to none," Robert answered with confidence, "but, of course, I'll only do it if the opportunity presents itself."

Jessica smiled and gave him a kiss.

"Just be careful."

"I will."

The two of them were like newlyweds, walking through multi-colored patches of leaves, holding hands, not saying much, just enjoying each other's company. Robert couldn't wait for Thanksgiving. It had been a while since he'd had so much to be thankful for.

Chapter 37

"Happy Thanksgiving, brothers. Welcome to this special meeting. I have coffee, cakes, and some leftover turkey for sandwiches when we are done," Arthur said, as the Council sat down in his living room once again—their new meeting place after they had discovered how much deeper their conversations went without the disturbance that was unavoidable in public spaces.

"Thanks, Arthur," Robert replied, "we are thankful for your friendship and hospitality."

"Hear, hear," Jack and George chimed in.

"Did everyone bring their quotes about love?" Jack asked, in his usual role as facilitator. They all nodded and he continued: "Okay then. I thought we might read our chosen quotes, say briefly what they mean to us and then have a short discussion about each quote. Who wants to start?"

"I'll go first," Arthur replied, grabbing the book beside him. "My quote is from Kahlil Gibran, who is one of my favorite authors. It goes like this: *When you love you should not say, God is in my heart, but rather, I am in the heart of God. And think not you can direct the course of love, for love, if it finds you worthy, directs your course. Love has no other desire but to fulfill itself.*"

For dramatic effect, Arthur paused and allowed the words to sink in.

"As you gentlemen know," he explained, "love is the centerpiece of my life. It wasn't always that way. In my twenties and thirties, I was angry and resentful, but thanks to my wife and to the people at Unity Church, I learned how to love, probably for the first time in my life as I can't say that I knew how to love before then. To me, this quote sums it all. Love is residing in the heart of God and when I surrender, I allow love to guide my actions."

"That's beautiful," George said, "but I don't quite understand. What's the difference between having God in your heart and residing in the heart of God?"

"To me, it is a matter of perspective," Arthur replied. "Having God in your heart summons a comforting emotion, but residing in the heart of God means that I surrender to the process and am enveloped by the energy of God. I see it as the difference between having a drop of love in my heart or being fully submerged in an ocean of love."

Robert wondered if Jack would interject, somehow lessen the power of the quote by dismissing the idea of God, but Jack stayed silent, and so did Robert.

"I like that," George replied. "Can I have a copy of that quote when we're done?"

"Of course," Arthur said. "Robert, can you gather all the quotes and send them to us in an email?"

Robert nodded and replied: "No problem."

"Anything any of you want to add before we go on to the next quote?" Jack asked. When no one replied, he continued. "Who's next?"

"I'll go next," George replied. Predictably, he had brought a Bible quote. It was Corinthians 13. He read: *Love is patient, love is kind. It does not envy, it does not boast, it is not proud. It is not rude, it is not self-seeking, it is not easily angered, it keeps no record of wrongs. Love does not delight in evil but rejoices with the truth. It always protects, always trusts, always hopes, always perseveres. Love never fails.*"

It was a beautiful verse, one that had been read in Robert's and Jessica's wedding. Listening to it brought back fond memories of promises made. Love does not envy, keeps no record of wrongs, is not easily angered. Tall words to live by. Robert had failed numerous times—as recent events had demonstrated—yet, he had also succeeded. Most importantly, he kept at it.

"And what does that mean to you?" Jack asked George after he finished reading the quote.

"I strive to adhere to these words in my life," George answered earnestly.

He was wearing a red Christmas vest over his usual white shirt and dress pant attire. All of the men were dressed up due to the holidays, except for Arthur, who always opted for comfort. He was wearing a tie-dye t-shirt inscribed with the words *Keep Austin Weird* and white hemp pants.

"I read the passage aloud to myself at least once a week and reflect on it—see where I am failing, where I am succeeding," George continued. "I also remind myself that the passage describes the type of love that God is continually showering on me. Only he fulfills every single promise made in that verse. It reminds me that even if I fail, the love of God never fails."

Robert listened. Still no jeer from Jack about God? What was going on? Had he suddenly changed his mind about being a proud atheist?

"I quite like that interpretation George," Arthur said in a thoughtful tone. "When I first read the Corinthians passage as a young man, I had problems with the absolutes, like the words, is, does, and always. I couldn't see myself as ever reaching the ability to love like that—not if I had to do everything that the passage described verbatim."

He cleared his throat and continued.

"Then, my friends at Unity helped me reinterpret the verse, framing it as a lifelong goal that I could continually strive towards. That way, I could keep those wise words in mind without feeling less than. Strange as it might seem, I had not thought about this passage as a definition of how God loves us until just now. Thank you George."

"So, you are okay with this passage—this list of promises that human beings can never achieve?" Jack finally asked. Here it comes, Robert thought, as Jack continued. "Don't you think that putting these insurmountable ideas in people's heads is tantamount to setting them up for failure?"

"Well, I think it's all a matter of perspective," Arthur replied. "For those of us who believe in the love and grace of God, the promises are fulfilled, just as George explained."

"But you hadn't thought of it that way until just now, had you?" Jack countered—evidently trying to be respectful, but disagreeing fervently. He continued without waiting for an answer. "I think that the passage is beautiful poetry, but as words to live by? Come on guys. People can't even live by the golden rule. How could they possibly live up to the Corinthians list?"

"Having aspirations doesn't have to be bad. We always want to be better than ourselves," Robert replied, thinking back to his own struggles with the idea of always getting better.

"Agreed. Aspirations can be good," Jack answered, "but a list of qualities that no human being has ever been able to display on a continual basis is the opposite of that. I mean, even Jesus failed to live up that list when he showed his fallible humanity a number of times according to the Bible. What I am saying is that people who try to live by such a celestial list either end up living in constant shame — embarrassed by the fact that they can't achieve whatever is being preached — or they just give up when they realize that they can never love like that, they stop trying."

Was there truth to what he was saying? Was this Bible verse actually setting people up for failure?

"What quote did you bring?" George asked Jack, clearly frustrated by the conversation that had been created by his favorite Bible quote of all time.

"I brought a quote from Friedrich Nietzsche," Jack replied. "It goes like this: *There is not enough love and goodness in the world to permit giving any of it away to imaginary beings.*"

Boom. He had dropped the hammer.

"To me," Jack continued, "it means that while other people are busy showering love on God, I'd rather shower love and goodness on the people who are around me. It's not necessary to look very far to see that people are not particularly good at loving each other, so I think that Nietzsche was right to say that there is not enough love and goodness in the world for us to use it so carelessly."

"Now wait a minute," the usually reserved George responded. "I find that showering God with love, and allowing God to shower me with love, makes all my relationships better, that I am more loving as a result. And honestly Jack, I don't see you displaying the loving kindness that you claim to show. If you were the most loving among us, the most generous, the most charitable, I would be inclined to agree with you, but you are not, as you just demonstrated by needlessly putting Arthur and me down for our beliefs."

Robert was impressed. George had finally stood up for himself. Instead of co-dependently trying to soften the situation, he'd said what was on his mind. And Jack was visibly startled. He had not expected that response from George.

After a moment of awkward silence, Robert turned to his friend and asked: "Why did you bring that quote, Jack?"

"To tell you the truth, I don't know," Jack replied, sounding both resigned and irritated. "Look, guys, I am sorry for insulting you, but for some reason, I knew that this love discussion would most probably end up revolving around God. For a person who doesn't believe in God, like myself, it's hard when a conversation endlessly revolves around what, to me, is essentially an imaginary concept. I just wanted to bring the discussion down to earth, that's all. Being offended can go both ways you know."

"My dearest brothers. God or not, we can be civil to each other. That is the central aspect of our covenant here in the Council," Arthur reminded them with his booming baritone voice.

"Of course, we can be civil," Robert added, "but we can also disagree, that is in our covenant as well. There is no animosity between us, right boys?"

"Right," George and Jack both replied in a dour tone—like two little boys who had just been told to be friends after a fist fight on the playground.

"The three of you know that I suffered a traumatic breakdown not too long ago," Robert continued, as the energy in the room settled down, "and that during that time, Arthur planted the idea of focusing on love in my mind. Thankfully, it has flourished ever since. It has changed my outlook on life. At the same time, I confess that I have not embraced the idea of God along with it. I am still an agnostic, haven't reverted to my Christian roots as he suggested. However, I have come to believe that love is a strong force in the universe—a force that might even exist outside of us. I believe that I can summon it, channel it, and dwell in it. I know it sounds corny, but believing in love helps me soften my imperfections. To me, that is the real power of love."

Robert took a deep breath and continued.

"In relation to our discussion, though, I feel there is more consistency between human ideas about love than there is about human beliefs about God. In that spirit, may I suggest that we focus on talking about love, leaving ideas about God to each of us, at least for now?"

"Agreed," Jack immediately replied.

"Agreed," Arthur and George reluctantly added in unison.

"Thank you. I must say that I didn't expect to be the level headed one here today, not with everything that has happened," Robert added with a chuckle, drawing a modest smile from each of the men.

"Getting back on track," Jack said, as he straightened his back and shifted slightly in his chair, "what quote did you bring Robert?"

"I brought two quotes from the Buddha," Robert replied. "The first one reads: *Hatred does not cease by hatred, but only by love; this is the eternal rule.* The second one reads: *You will not be punished for your anger, you will be punished by your anger.*"

Copying Arthur's approach, Robert paused for effect.

"I was being punished by my own emotions of anger, fear, and frustration. By focusing on love in all its shapes and forms—from the love that I have for my wife, to the love that I have for my children, to the love I have for life, to the love I have for nature, to the love I have for you guys, to even the strange kind of love that I have for my parents—I have been temporarily saved from myself, pulled back from the edge of what was essentially a nervous breakdown. My one realization is that love is not a destination, but a constantly renewed commitment. I must renew my willingness to live in a loving spirit every day, in the same way that I must take a shower every day."

Arthur smiled at Robert, knowingly, seeing how far he'd come in such a short time and said: "That is wonderful to hear brother. Love and light."

"You surprise me," Jack responded. "I was convinced that you were going to use Peck's definition of love that you always quote, you know, about love being the ability to sacrifice time, money and energy for another person's wellbeing."

"That is still part of my definition," Robert replied, "a part of my service orientation towards my family, but the reason I chose the Buddha quotes was that I have been so outwardly focused in my definition of love. Considering recent events, I needed love to win internally, to replace feelings of fear, anger, and irritation—you know, all the negative emotions that were tearing me apart—so these quotes spoke to me. In fact, I also found another Buddha quote that piggybacks on the two I have already used. It says: *Thousands of candles can be lighted from a single candle, and the life of the candle will not be shortened. Happiness never decreases by being shared.*"

Again, he paused for effect.

"That quote combines the previous two. Spreading happiness begins on the inside, by lighting your own candle. During my years in the therapy business, I have found that people who have a hard time loving themselves, have a hard time loving others. The golden rule begins on the inside."

"I like that," Jack replied.

Yeah, most atheists can find something in Buddhism they can relate to, Robert thought to himself. Buddhists don't have a centralized deity they worship.

"Yes, the Buddha, or the awakened one, was wise indeed," Arthur added.

New Agers like him as well, Robert thought as he smiled.

"Okay brothers, how do we tie a bow on this discussion?" Arthur said, getting ready to wrap up the meeting. "Any last thoughts?"

"Maybe our final thought should be that love isn't as complicated as we have made it out to be," the philosopher Jack said, after a short pause. "We like to philosophize, at least, I know I do, but when I have met parents who have caretaking instincts, like my wife or my friend Robert here, there is never a discussion about love, there is only action. At the end of the day, we can define love and argue about it, but maybe love is more an action than anything else. Do we act lovingly or not? To me, that is the central question, and I have to admit, that although my actions during this meeting may not have seemed very loving, I strive to act with love and compassion every day, to counter my intense intellectualism. The bow, for all of us to consider, especially me, is that love is action."

"That's about as good of a bow as you can put on a discussion," Arthur replied. "Love is action. What a great thought brother."

As the men devoured the turkey leftovers and cakes, they took turns asking Robert how he was doing and how everything was going at home. When he replied truthfully, that things couldn't be much better, each one of the men gave him a big hug and congratulated him. In their company, Robert truly felt appreciated and loved.

Chapter 38

When Robert closed his therapy practice in early November, he thought that it would take months for him to get a new job. That was why he was pleasantly surprised to get a phone call immediately after Thanksgiving in response to a resume he had sent in. The caller, a woman named Stacey Dickerson, offered him an interview with a leading Austin recovery program on the first of December. Lady luck was shining on him. He was in the flow. Good things were happening. A sign of that was that his entire family had been smiling from ear to ear as they had walked out the door earlier that morning. The air had somehow crisper, the colors more vibrant, each step they had taken a testament to loving life.

Have fun today Peter Pan, Jessica had said when he left for his interview, adding, you know, if the interview goes long, if they have more than one person interview you, then both of those are good signs.

Both had happened during the interview.

Robert felt like he had nailed it.

Of course, he had to admit that he didn't know what success felt like in this situation—he had not been through the job interview process since before he had gone back to school for his therapy degree—but he was optimistic. They were interested in him.

As he walked out of the building into the unusually chilly, wintery air, wearing his padded vest over a fleece jacket, he had to admit that he really wanted to work at this place. The potential for doing good here was much greater than it had been in his private practice. He could be helping alcoholics and addicts on a continual basis—every day. Plus, he could see himself riding the train to work every day and walking around downtown during his lunch hour, surrounded by life, not locked away in his office. He was excited.

Watch out for the highs and lows, an internal voice cautioned him.

It was true. Extreme highs and lows were his enemies. Not too happy. Not too sad. Equilibrium was his friend. Goldilocks was his role model.

"Love, grant me the serenity to accept the things I cannot change…" he whispered to himself as he got into his car. Love was easier to believe in than God. He had replaced the word, God, with the word, love, in each of the prayers he had been taught, both as a child and during recovery.

"The things I cannot change," Robert repeated out loud. He needed to accept every moment the way it presented itself. Que sera, sera. Whatever will be will be. Inhale light. Exhale love. If I get the job, great, he thought, if not, there is another job waiting for me out there.

He looked at the digital clock on the wood paneled Mercury dashboard. It was 11.30 AM. What to do with the rest of the day?

Well, at least, I don't have to torture myself thinking about marketing, he thought to himself as he smiled. No, now I'll just torture myself by thinking about whether or not I get the job.

Again, he focused on breathing deeply. Inhaling light. Exhaling love. He had just over three hours before the kids needed to be picked up from school. What should he do with that time? Go to his favorite downtown bookstore? Visit Whole Foods? Swing by the University to meet Jack? Go home early to snuggle with Jessica?

As he was getting ready to drive to his favorite bookstore, Robert was reminded of Dr. Vigo Andersen. The mental hospital was only a five-minute drive away. Should he visit? Not as a therapist, but as a guest? Why not? He needed to make amends. That would probably be the best use of his time. He could swing by the bookstore later. He changed direction and headed for the hospital.

On the way there, Robert had little time to think about what to do and what to say. He just wanted to clear the air. That was all. And he was curious. He wanted to see how Vigo was doing.

Before he knew it, he had found a parking spot directly in front of the mental hospital entrance. It's meant to be, he thought. He got out of the car, walked up the red stone path, opened the glass door and walked in to see his favorite receptionist, Amanda. Her warm smile greeted him.

"How are you today sir?" she asked.

"I am very well, thank you. How are you?" he replied, making her smile even broader. "I would like to visit with Dr. Vigo Andersen today if that is possible."

"Dr. Vigo Andersen, you said?"

"Yes."

"One moment sir," Amanda replied and reached for the phone.

Chapter 39

Andrew was deep in thought as he sat in his black leather chair and stared out the window of his second-story office. He was indulging in an emotion he rarely entertained. Regret. It had been three months since tragedy had struck and he blamed himself, felt that he could have done more, intervened sooner. Intellectually, he knew that regret was a useless emotion; that nothing could be done about the past; that what was done was done, but knowing that did not prevent him from periodically giving into the demands of the always present undercurrent of regret.

If only—that was regret's operative prefix.

If only he had done this.

If only he had done that.

Andrew leaned forward in his chair and grasped his full head of silver hair. His heart felt heavy. It reminded him why he shied away from deep emotional connections of any kind, why he had no wife and no kids. Emotional connections clouded his judgment and prevented him from acting professionally. He couldn't have that. He was a professional. That was his identity.

Andrew looked at the digital clock on his computer screen. The time was 11.42 AM. He would allow himself to wish for a better past for ten more minutes. That was all the time he allotted himself to be unprofessional—to be human. Then he would have to snap out it, straighten his tie, put on his white coat, and make the rounds.

"Dr. Burns? Dr. Burns?"

He was rudely interrupted when his assistant paged him over the hospital intercom. He'd expressly told her not to interrupt. He sighed. Good assistants were hard to find.

"Excuse me, sir," he heard her say in a muffled voice. "Amanda, at the front desk wants to speak with you. Says it's urgent."

He rolled his chair over to the desk and pushed the button on the intercom: "Karen, I expressly told you not to bother me except in the case of a medical emergency. Can't this wait?" he said. The sadness reverberated in his voice. Would she be able to sense it? He tried to straighten up, get himself into professional gear ahead of schedule.

"I am sorry sir, but she said it was urgent. I think you will want to take this call."

What could possibly be urgent that involved the front desk? Couldn't someone else handle this? Andrew felt a surge of irritation rising to the surface.

"Alright then. Patch her through," Andrew replied and picked up the phone.

"Dr. Burns?" Amanda's voice was both cheerful and concerned.

"Yes. This is him," Andrew answered.

"I am so sorry to interrupt sir. Karen told me that you were not to be disturbed, but I have a man here in the reception who is asking to see Dr. Vigo Andersen. I didn't know what to do, so I called you."

Vigo? Andrew sprang to attention.

"You did the right thing, Amanda. Did the man by any chance give his name?"

"Yes sir, his name is Robert Davis. He said he was here to see Dr. Andersen as a friend, not as a therapist, but considering… well, I just thought it would be best to call you, sir."

"Yes, of course," Andrew replied. "Thank you, Amanda. Will you tell him to wait in the foyer? I'll be right down."

Andrew stood up, put on his white coat, straightened his glasses and tie, and headed for the elevator.

"Cancel all my appointments for the rest of the day, Karen," he said as he walked passed his assistant.

He remembered Mr. Davis well. How could he not? Despite his obvious incompetence, Davis had been the one who got Vigo to talk. He had achieved a feat that had been beyond Andrew's ability. But why was he here now?

Bing. The elevator door opened. Andrew walked into the foyer and saw Mr. Davis immediately. He was sitting on an uncomfortable gray steel bench. When he noticed Andrew, he stood up and headed his way.

"Dr. Burns," Robert said, extending his hand. "I didn't mean to trouble you, sir. I just swung by to see Dr. Andersen. Last time I saw him, we didn't part on good terms. I wanted to see if I could patch things up. The lady at the reception insisted that I needed to see you first. Is there something wrong?"

Last time? Patch things up? What is he talking about? Andrew thought to himself.

"I am not here as a therapist, just as a visitor," Robert explained, responding to the puzzled look on Dr. Burn's face. "There is really no need for the two of us to talk unless you object to me visiting Dr. Andersen for some reason."

"I don't understand," Andrew responded. "What do you mean patch things up? We only asked you to come here once."

"Yeah, I know, but I saw Vigo, excuse me, Dr. Andersen, a few times after that, and the last time we met… look, there is no need to bother you, Dr. Burns. I just want to know if I can see him."

This man is delusional, Andrew thought to himself. There is no way that he could have seen Vigo since he came here the first time.

"Dr. Burns?" Robert repeated when he got no reply, "I must ask you again. Can I please see Dr. Andersen? Is he still here?"

"Mr. Davis," Andrew finally responded. "I must ask you to sit down. We have to talk."

They walked over to one of the gray steel benches, out of sight from the reception desk, and sat down side by side. It was now Robert's turn to look puzzled.

"Mr. Davis. I don't quite know where to begin," Andrew said. "There is evidently a great deal of misunderstanding that is clouding our communications, so let me try to be as clear as I can possibly be. First of all, I am afraid I wasn't exactly forthright with you when you came here back in September. Dr. Vigo Andersen wasn't just another patient. He was a good friend of mine."

"Was? What do you mean?" Robert queried.

"Please, allow me to explain without interrupting, Mr. Davis."

"I am sorry. Yes, of course."

"Yes, Vigo and I were best friends in college. Inseparable. That is until his mother committed suicide when we were nineteen. Hung herself. It was horrible. I blame myself, really. He pushed me away, but I should have stood by him, should have refused to leave his side."

Andrew's feelings of regret grew steadily as he spoke. He had not spoken of this to anyone, never revealed his connection. He'd only told the hospital staff that he had a particular interest in this case — instructed them to call him if anyone ever came looking for Vigo. That he was now confiding in Davis was somewhat baffling.

"We hardly ever spoke after that incident, so imagine my surprise when he entered my life again, this time as a suicidal patient. I swore that I would do all I could to save him, but I failed."

"What do you mean, you failed? He was alive a month ago, when I saw him last," Robert interrupted.

"That is unthinkable Mr. Davis. In fact, I can tell you, in no uncertain terms, that there is no way that you could have seen him more than once. You see, three days after your visit in September, my friend, Vigo, tried to kill himself again. He has been in a coma ever since. I failed him," Andrew said, talking to himself as much as he was talking to Robert.

"What you are saying is impossible, impossible I say," Robert replied frantically with an expression of disbelief. "I met Vigo several times after our initial visit. Several times. We spoke, just like you and I are speaking now. We spoke. There is absolutely no way that he has been in a coma. Do you honestly expect me to believe you? Is this some elaborate joke that you psychiatrists like to play on unsuspecting therapists like myself?"

Poor fellow, Andrew thought, now pulled out of his own feelings of remorse, fully engaged, observing what Mr. Davis was going through. He really believes that he met Vigo. He is delusional.

"Mr. Davis. Mr. Davis. Look at me," Andrew said firmly. "Calm down. I am not lying to you. This is not a hoax. Vigo has been in a coma for almost three months now. Whatever it is that you think you have experienced, I will help you through it. Mr. Davis. Please calm down. I will take you to see Vigo myself. We will work through this. You are okay, Mr. Davis. You are okay. Please, breathe."

Chapter 40

It was true. Robert could hardly believe his own eyes. There he was. Vigo. In a hospital bed. Tubes in his nose. His chest linked to a heart rate monitor that went beep every few seconds. His eyes closed. Nutrition being fed to him intravenously. Dr. Burns had been telling the truth. Vigo was in a coma. But how?

Beep. Beep. Beep. Beep.

Robert had been sitting in a chair next to Vigo's hospital bed for almost half the day now. He'd calmed down enough to call Jessica and ask her to pick up the kids, but he couldn't get himself to divulge what had happened. He hated himself for lying to her—especially since he'd promised to always tell her the truth not too long ago—but the implications were just too dire. Was he losing his mind? His interactions with Vigo had been as real as any he'd had over the past several months. Their conversations could hardly be ascribed to his imagination. No. Robert wasn't that good at imagining things. What the hell was going on?

After explaining what had happened, Dr. Burns had been meticulous in showing Robert the error of his ways. They had walked over to the reception desk and looked at the visitor logs. Robert had seen with his own eyes that he'd only been to the mental hospital once. Once. Come to think of it, Robert didn't remember his trips to and from the hospital. He didn't remember having any other interactions with the hospital staff. Yet, those doubts had not entered his mind in the past few months, probably because the interactions with Vigo had been so real. Dr. Burns had also shown Robert the admission records to the ER. There was no doubt. It had happened as Dr. Burns said. Three days after Robert's initial visit in September, Vigo had been rushed to the hospital. He had been in a coma for almost three months. Three months.

Now, Robert sat next to Vigo's bed, studying the old man, the heart rate monitor on the left side of his bed continuously beeping.

Beep. Beep. Beep. Beep.

"So," Robert said out loud, speaking to Vigo, even though he didn't expect to get a response, "your mom committed suicide, huh?" Robert cleared his throat. Those were the first words he had said for hours. His throat tickled.

"That explains a lot, doesn't it? Was that why you retreated into your own mind? Was that why you decided to escape life through your study and practice of meditation? I can see how that would work..."

The tickle sent Robert into a coughing fit. He coughed loudly, like a smoker grasping for his last breath of fresh air. When he gathered himself, Robert realized that Vigo hadn't been disturbed by the ruckus. Of course not. He was in a coma. Robert still couldn't believe it.

"That still leaves us with a big mystery Vigo, because your mom committing suicide doesn't explain why I've been having lifelike conversations with you while you were in a coma."

Robert sighed.

"Maybe I'm just koo-koo-crazy. That would explain other things as well… such as my emotional breakdown in October. Maybe I'm just losing my mind."

He chuckled nervously.

"Wouldn't that be a fitting end to the therapist who thought he could continually get better and better? If I am indeed crazy, that would be the incarnation of irony. They would have to update the Merriam-Webster dictionary, place a picture of me next to the word ironic and caption it with the phrase: He thought he could continually get better, but he was actually going off the deep end."

Beep. Beep. Beep. Beep.

"Is that all you can say, Vigo?"

Beep. Beep. Beep. Beep.

"You were much more talkative when you were in my imagination. Yeah, in my imagination. That's the only logical explanation for what happened, right? I imagined you. I projected, used your image to flesh out my fears about life and death. That's the shortest, simplest and most rational way to explain it. Except for one thing. I didn't know I had any of these ideas tucked away in the recesses of my mind. That's the part that I have a hard time understanding. I mean, Jack found your book, your book, which explained where you got your erroneous philosophy from, but that was after the two of us, me and you, had most of our discussions. That was your book, not mine. Your philosophy, not mine. I didn't even know about it until Jack handed me the copy, the one marked with your name."

Beep. Beep. Beep. Beep.

Robert was frustrated and confused. How could this be happening now, just when he had begun to piece his life back together? It seemed so unfair.

"The only other explanation I can think of is that you contacted me through some form of telepathy," Robert mused. "Aren't those the only two options, hallucination or telepathy? The latter would be better for me, right? Then I wouldn't be crazy. No, then I would be clairvoyant—a psychic—except, instead of being able to speak to the dead, I would only be able to talk to people who were in a coma. They'd call me the coma-whisperer. Do you hear how ridiculous that sounds, Vigo?"

Beep. Beep. Beep. Beep.

"No. Me going crazy is probably a better, more logical explanation, right? Although, I wish that telepathy was the answer, Vigo. I wish that you'd been talking to me."

Beep. Beep. Beep. Beep.

Robert looked at Vigo's ashen face. It seemed difficult to fathom that the rosy cheeks he had seen during their conversations had been... he didn't finish the thought. It didn't matter. It had all been in his head.

"I have a proposition for you, Vigo," Robert said, leaning in again. "I have heard that people in a coma can hear what is being said in their presence. If that is true, if you can hear me now, please, give me a sign. I beg you. Give me a sign that I am not crazy."

Beep. Beep. Beep. Beep.

"I am willing to accept anything," Robert added, "any sign will do."

Beep. Beep. Beep. Beep.

Robert looked around, at the silver-framed hospital bed, the green curtains, the leafless trees outside his window, the people rushing past him in the hallway, and then again at Vigo's comatose body.

There was no sign.

It was clear that he had hallucinated. That had to be the explanation.

Did that mean that other parts of his life were hallucinations as well? Could he be imagining his clients, his wife, his kids? Was it all one big dream, just like Vigo had said?

Robert pinched himself on the cheek. Aww! He took a large sip of water. It was warm and tasted like chlorine. His senses worked. He was not imagining this.

Beep. Beep. Beep. Beep.

"I give up," Robert finally said with a sigh. "You're not going to give me a sign, are you? You are in a coma. I am..."

Robert sat still, his arms hanging at his sides. His legs felt like they were bolted to the floor. He couldn't move. Sights and sounds were all but erased from his awareness. He just sat. Numb. Shocked. Immobile. He closed his eyes. Time came to a standstill.

Chapter 41

"Robert."

"Vigo? Is that you?"

"Vigo? Yes, you may call me Vigo, but it seems that you have learned very little from our interactions. You are still obsessed with the world of names and forms, still tethered to the dualistic and time bound version of reality."

"What? Are you dead? Is this a dream? Am I hallucinating again?"

"Reality is not a hallucination Robert. I am Real. I am that I am. Never born, will never die. My tether to the fragile body of Dr. Vigo Andersen will break soon. I only wanted to see if I could get through to you one final time."

"Okay, I'll play along with this hallucination. If you are Vigo's soul, why would you want to talk to me?"

"Because you are so close to uncovering the truth about life Robert. You are just about to unveil your primary reason for living and I want to help you. Also, I want you to know that Vigo's family history was what caused him to commit suicide, not his meditation practice. Through his meditation practice, he unveiled his true identity. His weakness, on the other hand, was due to his upbringing. The two had nothing to do with each other."

"How can you say that now? You have been telling me over and over again that you wanted to disrobe, that you were done with this body. Are you telling me that was a lie?"

"Yes and no. Vigo said that Robert. You have to understand that Vigo's mental state filtered my communications with you. Just as a ruby held to the sunlight makes the sun appear red, so did Vigo's mental and emotional state skew my communications. Only now, when Vigo's physical state is frail and his tether to me has weakened to a thread, can I can speak to you freely, without a filter. I can impart the knowledge that you so desperately seek."

"I don't get it. Why do you need Vigo's body to communicate with me in the first place? Why don't you just wait until his body is dead and then communicate with me unfiltered."

"Because that is not how it works Robert. Once Vigo's body is void of life, then I am freed into the ether. I become one with the universe, without form. There is no way to communicate with people who are working their way through the dream of life from a state of formlessness."

"There you go again, calling life a dream. I put it to you, voice that sounds like Vigo, that this, right now, this conversation, is a dream, a hallucination, an unfortunate residue of my nervous breakdown."

"It is regrettable that you see it that way Robert. Nevertheless, I will use this narrow window of opportunity to reveal the purpose of life."

"How am I supposed to respond to a dream that is telling me about the purpose of my life? It is ridiculous. I am ready to wake up now."

"All you have to do is listen, Robert."

"Do I have a choice?"

"Why are you so argumentative? Only a moment ago, you were begging for answers. Now that I am ready to give them to you, you reject the fact that we are even having this conversation. There is no effort required on your part. Just listen."

No response.

"I take your silence to mean that you are ready to listen and will proceed. The purpose of life, Robert, is to uncover the soul, to remember your real identity, to wake up from the dream of life."

"You have told me this already."

"Yes, but have you listened? Have you truly listened? No. You have squandered a golden opportunity by becoming obsessed with suicide. I have been trying to tell you this all along—even if it was through the limited means of Vigo's voice—but you have not listened. Let me tell you again. When a soul is born into this world, it forgets who it is and forms an attachment to the human body. In that bondage, it experiences a range of emotions—from fear to ecstasy—all of which it is unable to experience in its primal state. But, if the soul identifies too strongly with the body or mind, then life becomes a prison. Only by remembering its true identity can the soul transition back into the ether without passing through either heaven or hell first."

"Heaven or hell?"

"Yes, the stronger the bond that the soul has to the human body, thoughts, identities and range of emotions, the longer it spends prolonging that life in the mental space between physical existence and the ether, which is the void or emptiness from which the soul springs. This mental space, where thoughts and emotions carry on living, is called either heaven or hell depending on the life that a person has lived. Heaven is created by good attachments. Hell is created by attachment to fear, anger, hatred and so on."

"Pardon me Vigo's soul, but that is all bullshit!"

"I understand that having direct communications with me, without the filter of Vigo, can cause this reaction. This is a lot to absorb Robert."

"That's because it's bullshit. I don't care about heaven, hell, the soul, transitioning, or any of that shit. I want to live well. I want to be with my wife and kids. I want to serve people. That's all. I do not wish to uncover the soul."

"But you have Robert. You have. Through your meditation practice. Every moment of peace you have experienced is your essential state, your soul, the center from which all else springs. You are drawn to it because it feeds you, nourishes you. You call it being centered. You call it being focused. You call it being at peace. That is all that I am talking about. All you have to do is update your philosophy of life, allow it to reflect your experiences, know that you have uncovered your soul, and then live from that perspective. This will not cause you to want to die. It has nothing to do with that. Again, that part was all about Vigo's family history. Living from the perspective of the soul will not diminish your life, it will enhance it. You will feel more alive, more able to serve, more able to love. You will feel more, but it will bother you less. By acknowledging your soul, you will be living from a higher state of consciousness."

"Why can't I just have my moments of peace and be done with it? Why does it all have to mean something? You say that you want to communicate with me directly to help me, but all you have done is confuse me more."

"For now, it feels like confusion, but in ten years, twenty years, thirty years, when your body draws closer to its time of transition, then this knowledge will comfort you, give you peace of mind, allow you to live your life with more joy and less fear."

"It doesn't feel like that right now."

"I know and I am truly sorry for causing this temporary confusion, but in time, you will thank me."

"I am not so sure about that."

"I am."

"I just…"

"I know, but we must stop here. It is time for me to go now, Robert. Live well and remember who you really are."

Chapter 42

"Sir? Sir?"

Robert's body jerked as he regained awareness.

"Sir? We have already closed the hospital to visitors. You are welcome to come back tomorrow."

Beep. Beep. Beep. Beep.

"What?"

"Sir? Are you alright?"

"Huh? Yes. Who are you?"

"My name is Juanita Suarez, the night shift nurse. I am sorry sir, but I am going to have to ask you to leave. You can come back tomorrow. What is your name sir?"

"Huh? My name? Robert, Robert Davis."

"Well, Mr. Davis. You can come back tomorrow, but right now, you have to leave."

"Yes, of course," Robert said, rubbing his eyes. "Just give me a few minutes. I must have fallen asleep."

"That's quite alright sir. It happens a lot."

The nurse left the room.

Of course. The hospital.

Beep. Beep. Beep. Beep.

Robert was still in the hospital with Vigo. The breakdown had apparently affected him more than he realized. He had dreamt the whole exchange just now. The voice in the void. But, it had been so real, so vivid. The voice sounded just like Vigo.

You just experienced another hallucination, dammit, the reasonable voice in his head argued.

The reasonable voice? Was that also an illusion?

Whatever the case, it was clear that he would need more than just therapy sessions with Mrs. Goldberg. He was far gone. He probably needed meds. Maybe Dr. Burns could help him?

Robert shook his head and rubbed his face.

Beep. Beep. Beep. Beep.

"Hey, Vigo. You're still here. Didn't your soul say that it was time to transition?" Robert said, looking at the hospital bed that cradled Vigo's motionless body.

He stood up slowly. His back was aching and his legs felt like they were made out of wood after sitting for hours on end. He walked to Vigo's bedside and looked at him intently.

Of course, he was still alive. It had been an illusion, a dream, a delusion. To even consider that Vigo's soul had actually been talking to him...

Beep. Beep. Beep. Beep.

"Nope," Robert said. "It's all in my head. You are still in a coma. I am still hallucinating."

Robert forced a smile. The whole thing was ridiculous. If it weren't really happening to him, he would be laughing. But the smile was quickly erased from his face. His sanity was no joke. What would he say to Jessica and the kids? He had nearly lost them once. What would happen now?

I am sick, but I don't need to fix anything tonight, he reminded himself. The road to recovery is long. I only have to take one step at a time.

Even though he was parroting a twelve step phrase, he felt better. He was in shock. He needed some rest. He needed to go home.

Robert headed for the door. The light in the corridor had been turned down and he couldn't see any people moving around out there.

Looking back, he said: "Goodbye Vigo. I probably won't come and see you again. For what it's worth, I hope your transition goes well. This coma doesn't suit you."

As he turned around to leave, Robert was stopped in his tracks by a single sound coming from the machine next to Vigo's bed.

Beeeeeeeeeeeeeeeep.

No, it can't be.